The Mur

Lock Down Publicati

The Murder Queens 4

A Novel by Michael Gallon

Michael Gallon

Copyright © 2023 Michael Gallon

First Edition July 2023

Printed in the United States of America

Lock Down Publications
P.O. Box 944
Stockbridge, GA 30281
www.lockdownpublications.com

Like our page on Facebook: Lock Down Publications
www.facebook.com/lockdownpublications.ldp

Stay Connected with Us!

Text LOCKDOWN to 22828 to stay up-to-date with new releases, sneak peaks, contests and more…
Or CLICK HERE to sign up.

Like our page on Facebook:
Lock Down Publications: Facebook

Join Lock Down Publications/The New Era Reading Group

Visit our website:
www.lockdownpublications.com

Follow us on Instagram:
Lock Down Publications: Instagram

Email Us: We want to hear from you!

Chapter 1
Ten And A Half Inches!

Two hours later, the club was closing; Richard and I were still sitting at the bar waiting on the girls to dress in. Some of the females were leaving with us, while a few of the other girls had decided on leaving with their individual dates. Shortie had bounced back and made herself a few more dollars. Suga Bear, who I still say had something to do with her bag being missing in the first place, felt sorry for her and paid her bar fee while her sister, Chazz chipped in and gave her a few dollars as well. Due to her feeling sorry for her.

On the way out of the club, some lil female yelled out to the crowd. "Did somebody lose a purple Crown Royal Bag?"

Suga Bear looked back at Shortie while she was walking out of the club with Buster and fell down from laughing so hard at what the girl had just shouted out.

By now, all the girls with us knew that Shortie had lost her money bag. JK tapped Shortie on her back and whispered out loudly. "Man, that's so fucked up. She's probably the bitch who stole your bag!"

"Probably so, JK. It's all good. I know next time!" Shortie replied as we all walked out of the club together.

"Alright ladies, everyone to their individual vehicles."

"Hey, Mike, where are we having breakfast at?"

"We're stopping at the Waffle House back in Lakeland, Nicole."

We left Hollywood that night and headed back to Orlando. The females that rode with me were busy counting their money, while I was busy scheming on a plan for our next show. I was still thinking of how I could continue to keep everyone from finding out about me and the Murder

Queens, who were about to dispose of two crooked ass police officers.

The first thing that I had to do after we stopped at the Waffle House that morning was to calm down Ms. Nicole, who since she was riding in the front seat felt as though she was in charge of the group. I must admit, now that I was fucking her on a regular basis, she had all the right to feel like she was in charge. Besides when you were allowed to sit in the front seat next to me, you were looked at as the female who was definitely in charge and the female who was taking ten and a half inches of pure meat in between her precious legs daily.

On the way to the Waffle House, Nicole and I talked briefly that morning going back and forth about what she could do as far as being the leader of the dance group. But she had to keep our relationship business quiet. I didn't need anyone going back to Sharon with any information pertaining to Nicole and me. I also had to keep our business on the low low so that when Sexy Redd returned, she wouldn't hear nothing about what Nicole and I had going on.

While the ladies sat inside eating their breakfast, I was outside in my truck planning my next move. It was already around four thirty in the morning. By the time we would all get back into Orlando it would be daylight. So, I knew that I wouldn't have much time for any sleep when we all returned home. Needless to say, my two dear police officer friends were about to have an eternity of sleep, that neither one of them knew was coming.

Chapter 2
I Didn't Know!

My first order of business would be talking with my dear older brother about assisting with the disposal of the two crooked ass cops. They seemed to be popping up every time someone that I knew departed Yahweh's green earth.

Now two things for certain and one thing for sure about those two crooked ass cops, was that they really loved sleeping around with just about any female who would sleep with them for the right price. Now if my judge of character was correct, those two clowns would love to come out to witness my ladies performing at the Caribbean Beach night club on that beautiful Wednesday night.

It was the night that everyone in Orlando waited for and with the quick stardom my ladies were receiving, there was no doubt in my mind that those two wouldn't want to be at the spot with them.

So, with the help of my brother and them bad ass Murder Queens, that's exactly where they would be seen. After dropping off Mercedes and then Lil Kitty, I was headed home. I finally pulled through the guarded gate shack in Metro West around seven fifteen a.m. The local kids from the neighborhood were all waving and shouting good morning to me as I pulled onto my street. Once I pulled into my garage, I woke up the females that stayed with me.

Entyce, Strawberry, Nicole and of course the elegant looking, Mignon. There also was this one new cute chick that stayed with us by the name of Tameia who stayed down in Tampa that night with one of the Buc's players. Before leaving, she had assured me that she would be back in time for the show that night.

We all got inside right before the sun came up to shine throughout beautiful Orlando. With all of the girls still being somewhat sleepy, I decided that the time was at hand for me to discuss with them the plan of attack for my two police officer friends.

As we all walked inside of my den with a hot cup of something to wake us up with, my brother pokily walked in with a somber look on his face. I greeted him with, "Good morning, Firstborn."

He in turn looked at me with a defiant look and responded back with. "Morning to you as well Baby Boy."

Firstborn then looked over at the group of females, who called themselves the Murder Queens and smiled as he stared at Strawberry and the rest of them while uttering. "Ladies, it's such a pleasure to be amongst you all. I have heard so much about the skills that you all have."

"Hey, Firstborn," they all greeted him in unison as they sipped on their hot choice of something to help wake them up.

Firstborn then peeped over at Strawberry with his sadistic smile smeared across his wide ass face and said. "*Scrawberry*, how is that lil tight or should I say big ass pussy of yours doing this bright and early morning?" he asked as he slid his hand down to his crotch, while still having the sadistic smirk on his face.

The girls looked around at Strawberry and then back at my brother as Strawberry sarcastically replied, "It's doing just fine Mister Want to Beat up Some Pussy!" her face held a shitty ass smirk as she then took another sip of her steamy hot chocolate.

"Okay, listen up everyone, this is going to be short and sweet. I know that you ladies all want to get some rest before tonight's show. So, if you all let me do the talking, we can be done in an hour or so. Two of you young ladies will be performing in just a few hours, so time is of the essence."

"What does that mean, Mike?" Strawberry asked with a weird look on her obscure looking face.

"It means that time is not on your side," I replied as she looked over at Nicole, who was staring back at her as to say, *"Damn bitch!"* Strawberry glanced back at her and yelped. "Damn chick, I didn't know!"

Chapter 3
Smiling To Himself!

Nicole then averted her attention at me and muttered, "Go ahead, Mike, we're all good." She smiled as I happened to look down and notice that she sat there with her legs spread wide open without any panties covering up her lovely Hot Pocket. I gave her that quick Prince grin that I had mastered and started my meeting.

The plan was flawless and if everyone played their individual part to the T, not only would those crooked ass cops be dead and gone, but they would also be charged with the death of the other victims that had to be disposed of as well. My plan went something like this. First, Mignon would meet up with the two detectives at the leasing office for the homes out in Metro West at lunch time. That was the time that the real leasing officers took off for lunch. She would pretend to be the Property Manager and have the two idiots sign some fake ass ownership papers that would say that they were the proud owners of their own beautiful, lavish five bedroom four bath home, with a pool and spa along with the home being located next door to none other than Shaquille O'Neal, the starting center for the Orlando Magic. They would have to be there between the hours of twelve noon and one o'clock in order for the plan to be fail-proof.

The second phase of the plan would consist of the two of them traveling over to the Mercedes Benz dealership to meet up with Ms. Strawberry, who would be acting as the finance manager of the dealership, in which my brother would act as the salesman and sell them the automobiles.

Now the money that they had requested would come from the property room held at the police department in, which the female that I had met at Sharon's house on Sunday, worked at. Once the money was found on those two cops, the case would be solved.

After speaking with everyone for about two hours, we all adjourned off to our different areas of the house. It was somewhere around nine thirty and I couldn't wait to get to bed for some needed rest. But before I could doze off. I had to make a very important phone call to initiate the plan. The phone rang one time as Detective Protho answered.

"Detective Protho," he said as I cringed just hearing his voice, knowing that he was smiling on the other line knowing that it was me calling.

"Morning, officer."

"Ah, Mr. Vallentino, I didn't expect to hear from you so soon."

"I know I didn't expect my counterpart to give me all of the money this soon. But they, as well as I, wanted to get this matter dealt with as soon as possible."

"So, I take it that you have our money in hand?"

"Yes sir, and the deeds to the houses need to be signed between the lunch hour today. Not only can you guys look at your splendid homes between that time but you will be able to receive the keys to them as well."

"Wonderful, now what about those vehicles?" he asked as I could still picture the smirk on his face while he questioned me.

"The owner of the dealership would like for you and your partner to be there around four this afternoon so that you all can pick out the ones that you want and have them customized to fit your needs. You all will also have to fill out the necessary paperwork so that the vehicles can be placed in your names. So, please make sure that you guys have the right identification along with your bank account statements."

"Now that's what the fuck I'm talking about, a brother who works fast on his feet," Detective Protho replied while standing up from his desk, rubbing his hands together and smiling to himself.

Chapter 4

Scrawberry!

Now after I had done all of that, here is where the plot thickened.

"Oh, by the way before I forget, since we were closing out our deal today, I thought that it would be nice to invite you two fine officers of the law out tonight for some adult entertainment."

"Sounds good, what did you have in mind?" He asked.

"Well, you know that I have my females and about fifteen more females dancing at the Caribbean Beach Club tonight, inside of Disco's Boom, Boom, Room?"

"Now that sounds like it will be a lot of fun."

"What's that partner?" Detective Pass asked Protho in the background ear hustling.

"Mr. Vallentino has our packages and is inviting us to come out to the club tonight for some VIP treatment."

"What, that fast? You mean to tell me that he has already came up with all the money?" Detective Pass asked as he stood up thinking about all the money he was about to get a hold of.

"Yes, and on top of that, he is inviting us out to the club tonight to celebrate with him and his crew of beautiful exotic women," Detective Protho said to his partner, just as he turned to speak back into the phone with me.

"So, what time should we be ready tonight, Mr. Vallentino?"

"The ladies and I won't get there until around eleven thirty tonight, just give me your address and I'll have one of the limo drivers to pick the both of you guys up along with two beautiful women inside of the limo for your personal dates."

"Sounds like a plan, Mr. Vallentino, but what dates?" he asked, sounding too concerned.

"My bad, I'll be sending to of my finest women along with the limo to escort you guys to the club tonight. And before it slips my mind, your money will be inside of the limo as well," I replied now with my evil smirk across my face.

"Mr. Vallentino, I must admit, you really know how to make a guy feel good about himself. After tonight you will be a friend to my partner and I for life!"

"My sentiments exactly," I replied to the detective as I wiped the devilish grin off my face.

"We'll see you tonight, have a nice day, Mr. Vallentino."

"You certainly will my fellow friend." I hung up the phone with the detective while my brother sat there shaking his head.

"Damn, Baby Boy, you must want to really get rid of those two crooked ass cops mighty bad?" First born asked me as he sat there listening to the end of my conversation with the detective.

I sat down as I looked him directly in his eyes and muttered, "Yes sir, the quicker we do this, the better I will sleep at night!"

My brother leaned forward and clasped his hands as he looked at me sitting across my walnut stained desk. "So, do you want me inside the limo tonight with the driver?"

"Nah," I quickly responded. He seemed puzzled as he looked at me with a quizzical look upon his face.

"Well, where am I gonna be, with you?"

"Nah, your ass is going to be the one driving the limo. It's the same limo that those two clowns are looking for. And oh by the way, your name tonight is Larry. Also please don't let me forget to give your ass that Jamaican wig too. Once you bring them to the club, then you will post up with me surveying the club."

"Cool Baby Boy, but what about me at the dealership?"

12

"Nigga that's why I'm giving your simple minded ass the wig, so you can look completely different tonight," I said as I stood up from my desk.

"My bad, is there anything else, because if you don't need me anymore I'm about to go dig off into some more of ol' Scrawberry," Firstborn replied while grabbing his manhood and displaying a fucked up ass grin on his face as if he already knew that he was about to fuck the shit out of poor old *Scrawberry* as he called her. Since his country talking ass couldn't pronounce the word Strawberry.

Chapter 5
Smooth!

Firstborn was just about to walk out of the room when I stopped him with. "Oh yeah, one more thing that I forgot to tell you."

He turned back towards me smiling and eagerly wanting to go tear a hole in poor ole Strawberry.

"Rhynyia's family is flying me down to Puerto Rico next week. I'm going to need you to accompany me, so that you can watch my back while I'm down there."

"Say no more Baby Boy, it would be my pleasure to come with you down to Puerto Rico."

I stood up walking towards him standing at the entrance of my den. "Firstborn, one thing though."

"Yes, what is it Baby Boy?" he asked as his smile disappeared.

"Promise me that you will not get involved in her father's business."

He seemed puzzled as he looked back at me and asked. "Why would you say that?"

I placed my right hand on his broad shoulder and replied, "Just know that her father can be very influential when it comes to doing what he does."

He was now looking me directly in my eyes when he said to me. "May I ask you what it is that he does, Baby Boy?"

I smirked as I stated, "He's in the illegal drug trade business, my foolish older brother."

He then placed his hand under his chin. "Oh I see." He then winked his eye at me and walked out of my den.

Little did I know at that very moment, he would end up doing so much business with Pierre Santiago that they would have to come up with a new law just to stop him. After the large amount of Colombia's purest white powder known to man as Cocaine, the Feds changed his government name to Smooth. For him being that smooth in evading and eluding capture.

After sleeping for a few hours, I was off to the leasing office to watch Mignon in action with my two crooked police officers. I stood back and watched the both of them come into the leasing office bragging and being all arrogant as they talked amongst themselves. But when they saw Mignon, both of their beady eyes lit up like a Christmas Tree. They started telling Mignon how they wanted different portions of their houses changed once they moved in. Mignon was playing her part to the T while looking like a professional businesswoman at the same time. I got turned on just by standing behind the glass window watching her place the fake leasing documents in their faces to sign.

Three hours later, the two dumb founded officers of the law were at the Mercedes Benz Dealership with my brother pretending to be their salesman. Meanwhile, I was off inside of the finance office looking at how easy it was for him to convince those two clowns that they were about to be proud owners of their own Black Big Body Mercedes Benz.

While I was standing there, I overheard one of the salesmen. "Hey, who is the new black guy out there with two customers already," the tall white salesman said to his short, pale, white counterpart.

"Oh him, he's supposed to be here from the Corporate Office just showing off the new six series," I said to the two white salesmen as they both stood there sipping on their coffee.

I was in awe as I watched how smooth Firstborn looked as he made their job look easy.

"Hell, we're both glad that he doesn't work here. As good as he is laying it on those guys out there, he would be top salesman around here in just a few days," the tall thin salesman by the name of John said to me while the other pale faced one, by the name of Timothy, both stood there laughing at what John had just said to me.

Chapter 6

Thirty-Six B!

I then smiled at the two unwittingly salesman, while watching my brother continue to fool Detective Protho and his partner. After a few minutes of me standing there in the window, I walked back inside the finance office to check on Strawberry, who was sitting at the desk with a bright professional smile on her cute face.

I poked my head inside and asked her. "Are you okay?"

She looked up at me from her makeshift desk with a stern look on her face. "Mike, I got this," she replied as she placed a pair of reading glasses on her face, to help throw off her appearance.

"I know you do, girl. I'm just making sure that you like your new desk?"

"Whatever Mike, this is not something that I think that I would like to be doing."

"I know, you like eating the dick off of the bone," I replied while cutting a smile back at her.

She quickly snapped back with. "Boy, shut up and if your wild and crazy ass brother keeps beating up my lil twat-twat, I'm not going to be able to dance. He has my lil red ass sore right now," she said to me as I saw Firstborn and my two friends walking through the side door of the building.

"Sorry to hear that. I'll see you back at the house. Berry and I'll speak to my brother about your lil twat-twat being sore later. Peace," I said to her as I hurried through the front door, while placing my shades over my face ready to get back home.

Now that everything was set in motion for tonight, I was off to the house to prepare for my best performance ever. For tonight would be the final chapter in my life when it came to dealing with them two crooked ass cops.

I walked back inside of my house around six fifteen as the aroma of some Caribbean cuisine caught my nose and wouldn't let it go. At first, I thought that maybe it was my empty stomach playing tricks on my nose, but the closer that I got to my kitchen, I knew that my nose wasn't lying to my stomach. I bent the corner of the kitchen to see my girl, Tameia doing what she did better than having sex. Cooking.

"What time did you get in, beautiful?" I said to her as she turned her small body frame around to me.

"I got in around two thirty and couldn't sleep, so I decided to cook everyone some dinner before we had to leave for the club tonight."

"Sounds good to me. What are you cooking?" I asked her as I walked over to the fridge for something to drink.

She turned her head towards me as she replied. "Well, you know since I have a lil Caribbean in me, I decided to cook some Curry chicken with some rice and peas, along with some cabbage and some cornbread. Oh and a few Plantains also," she said to me as she stood there in a nice tight fitting pair of her Florida Hot Girls biker shorts, with her Florida Hot Girl T-shirt to match.

Tameia was picture perfect as she stood there talking to me in her Caribbean accent. You see Tameia was just the right addition to the group. She stood five foot four, weighing somewhere around a hundred and twenty-seven pounds with a nice, elegant bright red skin complexion. She had a nice set of full lips that were aligned on her lovely face perfectly. Her chest size had to be at least a thirty six B, as she stood there with her cleavage showing and my eyes watching.

18

Chapter 7

Always, Say No More!

When Tameia first came to the group, some people would mistake her for a shorter version of Megan Good but to me, she was just my Caribbean Princess. As she stood there with her lil phat ass poking out of her shorts, I smoothly walked over and kissed her ever so gently on her cheeks as I mumbled into her ear. "Now that's what the fuck I'm talking about. How long before dinner is ready?"

She looked up into my face with her radiant smile and uttered, "In about another thirty minutes, Michael."

"Okay, please call me when it's ready," I said to her as I turned to walk away.

"No problem, Michael," she shouted as I went to walk upstairs to my room.

While slowly walking upstairs I could hear some Jaheim slowly playing from one of the rooms upstairs. The song was Ready, Willing, and Able. The closer I got upstairs, I realized that the music was coming from non-other than my master bedroom. I sluggishly opened the door to find Ms. Nicole laying there butt naked in my bed with her legs wide open and pretending to be fast asleep.

I sat on the edge of the bed trying to take off my Stacey Adams when she dully rolled over and placed her hand on my back.

"So, you're going to just sit there and pretend that you don't hear what Jaheim is saying to you. young man?" She mumbled with the smell of peppermint on her breath.

"Damn, I thought that your fine lil short ass was sleep and yes, I hear what the man is singing. Now what?" I replied as she took my head and turned it to face her. Then, she placed her luscious soft lips of hers on mine and inserted her tongue down my throat. At the same time, she was unzipping my tailored fitting slacks. I heard them hit the floor as she reached inside of my sports briefs and grabbed a handful of my manhood. She slowly started stroking it up and down trying to get me aroused. Within minutes, she had me standing there rock hard with both of our lips locked. At first, I tried to resist her temptation, but as we all know, she was too strong for my weakened will power.

After she saw how hard and thick she had my manhood, she quickly pushed me down on the bed and slid her lil fine butt naked ass right down on it. Before I knew it, the poor lil female had all ten and a half inches of my rock hard manhood immersed in her small body frame. I could feel her wetness as she started riding me as if she was actually riding a wild stallion.

She was trying to take all of me at one time, as I grabbed her by her small waist and started pulling her up and down on top of my Mandingo. She began making crazy fuck faces as I went deeper and deeper into her womb. I was so deep that I could see the walls of her stomach move as my manhood was going up and down inside of her tiny ass stomach. She was grimacing and looking like she was in pain when I asked her.

"Are you alright or do I need to ease up a lil bit?"

She stuttered as she replied back with, "No it's fine. If you keep making love to me like this, maybe I could get used to Mandingo." She then continued to take all that pure pressure that I was putting her lil small ass through.

We both were off in the moment when the song by Nivea came blasting through my sound system. The song was 25 Reasons. It sounded so damn nice as she was trying to position herself so that she could enjoy all of me inside of her. She then fell down on top of me as she whispered into my right ear. "Oh shit, that's my song!"

I then bit her on her earlobe and uttered the same damn thing, while holding onto her and pumping her as if I hadn't had any sex in two years.

After another thirty minutes, sexy ass Nicole was having her third orgasm, while staring directly into my eyes and smiling at me as she laid there on top of me sweating.

I then pulled my manhood out of her tight feeling vagina, laid her on her stomach, and whispered, "You don't mind if I hit you from the back, do you?"

She looked back at me with one tear snaking down her face and replied, "No, Michael, just be gentle!"

My reply was, "Always, say no more, baby girl."

Chapter 8
My Baby!

Every time I pushed forward, she was pushing back, while being in sync with my motion. She then put an arch in her back as she turned her head around to see the expression on my face. She let out a lil moan as she saw the look on my face. I was trying to blow her back out since she had begged me to make love to her.

"Michael, Michael!" she screamed. As soon as I heard my name being called out, it was all over for me. I had nutted so damn hard, as I was trying to pull out of her at the same damn time. But her lil grown ass insisted that I cum inside of her.

Once she felt as if I was done, she then took the rest of my rock hard manhood out of her warm vagina and placed it inside of her mouth and began sucking the remaining juices that were coming out of my manhood. It looked like she was drinking water from a garden hose, as she held on tight to the base of my manhood.

She then looked at me and said the oddest thing ever. "Michael, since I can't have all of you, half of you will do just fine." she then smiled and stood up to walk into the bathroom.

I quickly jumped up and yelled. "What did your lil freaky ass just say Nicole?" I could hear the shower come on as she closed the door to my bathroom.

While she was in the shower, I just stood there staring into the mirror thinking to myself. *'Man, I hope this chick isn't trying to get pregnant by me.'*

Then I started thinking. Hell, she wasn't fucking anyone else but me, so if she did become pregnant I would be having three fucking babies around the same damn time.

I rushed into the bathroom to catch her standing there looking in the mirror at herself while the shower was running. I gently placed my hand on her shoulder and asked her. "Nicole, what's wrong, is everything okay?"

She looked up and stared me directly in my brown eyes and sputtered. "You heard me, Michael. If I can't have all of you, I would gladly settle for having a part of you inside of me!"

I quickly shot back at her with. "C'mon, Nicole, you can't be serious."

"That's where you're wrong, Michael. I don't want to be dancing all my life. I want a family of my own one day. And I have been wanting to have your child since the day that you took my virginity. Listen to the song that's playing on your sound system, Michael. That's how I feel right about now," she said to me as she stepped into the shower with Luther Vandross playing in the background. The song was If Anyone Had A Heart. As she abruptly closed the shower door, I could only think to myself. *'Why would this chick want to have my baby?'*

Chapter 9
Nothing To Worry About!

An hour later, we were all seated around the dinner table eating some of Tameia's Curry Chicken.

"Damn, this food tastes better than the food we ate at the restaurant the other day!" Entyce voiced as she stuffed some more cabbage down her throat.

Mignon and Strawberry sat aside her trying to finish off their food so that they could change out of their clothes from earlier.

"So, how did everything go today ladies?" I asked as I sat there enjoying our dinner.

"Everything went as planned Mike, without a hitch. I have all of their personnel information along with some of their most up to date bank account statements," Mignon said as she sipped on her cold glass of iced tea.

"Sounds good. Okay ladies, you all have to get ready for tonight's final performance."

Just as soon as I said that, the doorbell rang.

"Ump, I wonder who that could be?" Tameia recited as she pushed her chair away from the table. "Y'all go right ahead and eat, I'll get it."

I couldn't help but watch her nice fine portioned body walk away to answer the door, while Nicole felt different about me staring at Tameia's fine body.

"Alright Michael, keep them eyes in your damn head before I take 'em out!"

"Damn Nicole, I can't admire the fine specimens that I have working for me?"

She dropped her fork in her empty plate and replied with a hint of jealousy in her voice, "Hell nah, because if you start to stare hard enough, you might want to see just how nice her ass is!"

"Ump, I guess you heard that Mister Hoe ass Michael Vallentino!"

"Whatever, Strawberry." I replied as Tameia came back into the dining room with Ms. Tamika.

"Excuse me, Mike, Ms. Tamika is here to see you."

I turned around to see Tameia and Tamika standing behind me with a bright smile on her face and a black brief case in her hand.

"Hello everyone," she said to the ladies as I quickly stood up from the table, wiping my hands on my napkin.

"Hello," they all said in unison.

"Hi, Tamika, is that what I've been waiting on all day?"

"Yes, Michael, " she replied as she continued smiling at me and the ladies.

"Excuse me ladies while I speak with Tamika in the den." I then excused myself from the table as I placed my napkin on the finished portion of my Curry Chicken that I had in my plate. I then took Tamika by her hand that was empty and led her into my den, to discuss the business at hand.

Nicole, who was still feeling some type of way about the way I was looking at Tameia, sat still at the table with her eyes trained on me and Tamika walking away.

"It was nice meeting you ladies," Tamika shouted as she walked away.

"Same here, Tamika," the ladies responded as they all watched Tamika's nice ass hips sway from side to side.

"Damn Nicole, if your eyes could burn a hole in someone's back, you would have set ole girl on fucking fire," Strawberry said to Nicole who had got up from the table, walking towards the sink with her empty plate.

"Shut the fuck up, Strawberry. I'm not in the mood right fucking now!" Nicole replied as Entyce and Mignon looked over at Strawberry, who was wiping the smile off of her face and said, "Damn bitch, I was just teasing your lil sensitive ass!"

"Ladies, ladies, what's all the fuss about?" Tameia asked as she began clearing off the table. "Does anyone want seconds, and what do y'all have going on? Did I miss something?" She asked the room of females in her Caribbean accent.

"Nah, I'm good," Nicole said to her as she walked back upstairs to her room, so that she could get ready for her performance.

"No Tameia, you didn't miss anything. We just have something important to do tonight. That's all, nothing to worry your pretty head about," Mignon said as she placed her plate in the sink and walked upstairs.

Chapter 10

What Daughter?

Just as Tamika and I had reached the doorway to my den she stopped and looked and me and recited. "So Michael, you never told me that you lived with a house full of gorgeous women and not to mention they cook for you as well!"

I was just about to sit down at my desk as I replied back with, "Well you never asked. You left so fast the other day that you didn't give me a chance to let you know of my job change."

"I must admit there, Mister Michael, it looks like you're doing mighty damn good for yourself," she said to me as she cut a cute devious smile my way while still looking around at her elegant surroundings.

"It pays the bills, young lady."

"I see," she replied.

"I'm glad that I remembered your number," I said to her as I got comfortable inside of my chair.

"Yeah, I'm glad that you did too. Once I seen my two dick head co-workers show up at Sharon's house, I knew that it was time for me to leave; They're not going to miss this money, are they Michael?" She asked me as she placed the heavy black briefcase on my desk.

"Not at all, beautiful. Once the play goes into effect, the money will be all accounted for."

"But what I want to know is how are you going to make this shit stick on them two?" She asked with a quizzical look on her puzzled face.

"You let me worry about that, Tamika. Just know that after I get through with these two crooked ass cops tonight, part of your family will be set for life."

"So, Mike, your telling me that those two cops had something to do with my cousins death as well as my uncle disappearing?" She asked as she sat down on her voluptuous Gold Mine.

For a second there, her question caught me off guard. I then looked away from her because I couldn't stand to look in her eyes and lie to her at the same time. So I answered her with, "Yes, and I'm about to expose their entire crooked ass plan to extort me for my money as well," I replied as I stood up and walked her back out of my den, headed back downstairs.

Once downstairs, she said goodbye to the remaining girls as she walked past them still in the dining room talking about all the money that they were going to make at the Caribbean.

We had just walked outside as she opened the door to her brand new black Honda Accord, when she turned to me and asked, "So does my cousin Sharon know about all these beautiful half naked ass females you have living with you?" Her face held a wicked smile as she placed her soft, fat ass down in her car seat.

"Yes and why do you ask?" I said to her as I closed the door to her car.

"Because if you were my ol' man, you wouldn't be in that nice ass house with all of them fine young ass females," she replied as she rolled her eyes back at me.

"That's one thing about Sharon that I like."

"And what's that playa?"

"She knows that I don't keep any secrets from her," I replied as she started her car and then looked up at me and said.

"Well, I guess our secret is safe with me about our past relationship."

"Damn Tamika, how long ago was that again?" I said to her as I stood there smiling and bumping my hands together as we talked with one another.

"It was just a few years ago, Michael, but that still doesn't mean that you can't come see your daughter every now and then." She placed her Gucci shades on her face as she rolled up the window.

My heart stopped as she began to back out of my driveway.

"Tamika, what daughter?" I screamed to her as she backed out.

She then placed her car in drive and blew the horn twice as she drove away, with me still saying to myself, *'What daughter?'*

Chapter 11
Ate Out Earlier!

As time continued moving, the house grew larger with females as most of them decided to come by and get dressed for the club. In the end, that would be one of the worst mistakes of my career by letting people know where I laid my head at night. I should've learned my lesson the night that those characters tried to rob the girls and I. But no, I kept right on letting people know where I lived, something that I would learn to regret some nine years later, when one of my closes relatives would almost lose his life because of people knowing where we lived. Something that still haunts me till this very day.

When I finally got downstairs, most of the ladies in the group were all finished and ready to leave for the club. We had a brief meeting of what I expected of them that night. After the meeting, we all took off for the club.

Everybody except Nicole and Entyce. It was their time now for their performance. They rode in the limo with Firstborn so that they could pick up Detective Protho and his partner.

Meanwhile, on the way to the club, Tameia was busy telling the ladies that her friend from the Buccaneers and a few of his teammates were coming to the club to throw major money their way. If they wanted to be participants of the big dollars to have their game on tight.

Firstborn had just got to the hotel where the two officers wanted to be picked up at. He was standing outside of the limo as he greeted both men. "Good evening, gentlemen," Firstborn said to the two men as he opened the rear passenger door of the nice plush limo.

"Thank you my good man," the officers stated as they entered the limo. Their eyes enlarged bigger than freshly made silver dollar pieces when they laid eyes on Nicole and Entyce who were sitting inside the limo waiting on them.

"Now this is what I'm talking about. Some fine ass butt naked hoes along with some nice ass Crown Royal to get a brother in the mood for fucking!" Detective Pass shouted in excitement as he sat his tall lanky ass down beside Nicole, who barely had on any clothes.

"And what is your name beautiful?" Detective Protho asked Entyce, who was sitting there with a glass of bubbly in her hand.

"They call me Entyce, but tonight, Big Daddy, you can call me whatever your heart desires to call me, with your sexy ass." Entyce smiled as she replied to Detective Protho, who was sitting there rubbing all over her big soft luscious titties.

"Damn man, as fine as these two lovely ladies are, we don't need to go to the club. We should just stay right here at the hotel and get our freak on," Detective Pass uttered, while sipping on a glass of the spiked Crown Royal and licking his big ass crusted lips.

Firstborn heard him utter those sentiments as he fleetly slammed the car in drive and darted to the club, knowing that the plan was for him to bring all of them to the club.

Detective Pass was so baffled at the nice camel toe protruding through Nicole's black see through lingerie outfit that he started stuttering thinking about how nice it would be to be sucking on the lips of all that sitting between her thighs.

"Girl you make my wife look like a bowl of hot dog shit, as fine as you are looking tonight. You so damn fine that I would lick the crack of your beautiful, red, nice round ass after you have had a bowel movement!"

Nicole almost threw up in her mouth, due to the foul stench coming from his mouth.

Without thinking, she utterly replied, "Hell, your mouth smells like you already have been eating out of some nasty bitch's ass already!"

His head snapped up as he said, "Excuse me, what did you just say?"

Entyce quickly cut in with, "Nothing, she said that could she have a piece of gum because her breath smells like someone's ass already!"

Nicole cut her eyes over at Entyce and sputtered, "No I didn't, Entyce. I said that his breath already smells like he has been eating up in a bitch's ass!"

Entyce just put her head down in her lap and mumbled to herself. "Man, this bitch is going to get us both killed."

That's when Detective Pass said, "Oh my bad, my mouth probably does smell a lil foul. I had ate out my wife before I got to the hotel."

Chapter 12

As Fate Would Have It!

Nicole quickly looked over to Entyce and shouted. "See Entyce, I knew I wasn't tripping. This niggas mouth, smells like a full pot of fucking stank ass chitterlings!"

Detective Protho then threw a peppermint over to his tall, stank breath partner as he recited, "Oh yeah partner I meant to tell you about your shitty ass breath earlier. I just thought that you had passed gas or something. That's why I hesitated to say anything to you about it."

Detective Pass looked sad as he voiced back. "Nah man, I've been telling my ole girl that she needs to go have her shit checked out by her doctor, but she always says that she will just douche like that will kill the smell. But as usual, her shit always be smelling rank and shit. No matter what she does to her nasty smelling ass pussy!"

As he was sitting there talking about how stank his wife's pussy was, Nicole was busy trying to keep herself from throwing up all over her outfit, while Entyce was sitting in her seat rolling with laughter.

After about ten minutes of listening to Detective Pass complain about his ladies stank ass pussy, Nicole blurted out.

"Stop it, I say."

She couldn't bear to hear any more about his wife. She was so aggravated with the presence of this man that every time he touched her, her skin would crawl.

When Richard and I arrived at the club with the other ladies, he led them inside the club through the side door entrance, so that they wouldn't have to wait in the long line of people.

I pretended that I had left something of importance inside of the truck, when I shouted out to them. "Hey, I'll meet you guys inside." As soon as I had shouted out my intentions, the limo was pulling up just in time.

Firstborn saw me standing off to the side of the building dressed in my black Brooks Brothers suit. I motioned for him to circle the parking lot twice, so the people in line would think that it was some big time rapper or star inside of the limo. With the way my brother had that limo looking, all I could do was smile at the attention they were receiving.

When the occupants of the limo stepped out, it only signified what everyone was thinking as it made the two detectives look like they were some real big name players, especially with the way Entyce and Nicole turned heads with what they both had on their nice ass bodies.

I was still standing near the entrance of the club, taking everything in. It kind of brought a smile to my face to see how they had them two non—dressing ass niggas looking. With the way Nicole walked by me and winked her eye, it led me to only believe that everything was okay as her and her date walked into the club hand and hand. Her nice black see through outfit would have made any man lust for her sheer presence around them with the way she was strutting her stuff that night.

Meanwhile, Entyce had on some nice tight ass Apple Bottom jeans along with a nice Apple Bottom shirt and bra that was holding up those nice ass melons that she had on her chest. In other words, her titties were mouthwatering as she walked by me. I mumbled to myself as my girls walked by me looking flawless. *'Damn, both of my Nubian Princess were looking good enough to eat.'* and that's exactly what them two dick heads thought that they were going to do after the club. But as fate would have it, there was something else planned for the both of them that night.

Chapter 13
Dirty Redd!

I walked inside and the club was packed as usual. The Boom Boom Room was getting set for another off the chain show, with me and the Florida Hot Girls. I must admit, the Caribbean Beach Nightclub was one of my most profitable spots that I had ever had, past and present. But on this particular night, I was about to lose one of my most prized possessions, along with two cops giving up their crooked ass lives so that I could continue my life without them ever looking over my shoulders again.

As I walked in the room where the ladies were dressing in, JK stepped up to me with, "Mike, where have you been? We have been looking for you everywhere?"

"JK, you could have gone to Richard with whatever you needed."

"Oh no, Mike, he is not our manager and besides, he be acting like he don't know nothing when we ask him a question."

I was standing there laughing as she continued talking in her lil squeaky voice when Protho and Pass came strutting through the door with my ladies on their arm. I could tell that they were half drunk by the way their words slurred off of their tongues and by the way they were walking.

As they stumbled through the club doors, they saw me standing there talking with JK.

"Mike man, you really know how to treat your friends. When does the rest of your fine stable of women come out, or better yet, when do they start taking off their clothes?" Protho asked as he could barely stand on his two feet.

"You two go ahead inside. We have a special VIP section set up for you guys along with your lady friends."
They walked in the direction of the Boom Boom Room.

Firstborn walked up to me from behind. "Baby Boy, those two clowns right there have to be the two corniest ass cops that I have ever seen. Them silly ass niggas didn't even ask about their money that's still sitting in the back of the limo."

I turned to face him as I replied, "Damn, to busy trying to look at some pussy. Let me have around five stacks out of the briefcase, so that I can give them some money to throw at the ladies!"

"Alright, I'll be right back." Firstborn went to walk out of the door when I shouted out to him,.

"Hey, take this pass so that they don't stop you when you try to come back inside."

"Thanks, Baby Boy, I'll be right back!"

"I know you will, with all this pussy up in here to-night," I said to him with a million dollar smile on my face.

You see by now I had about twenty-five girls dancing inside of that club. And not to mention the females that my good friend, Money from Tampa was bringing. I think the name of her ladies were called The Ladies of Seduction, or something like that. Whatever it was, they were so damn fine that I wanted to change the name of my girls.

Now even with what I had going on, I still called on my nigga who had gave my ladies there first big break at Apollo South. His name was O.J.. and he was bringing one of the baddest females you had ever seen from Tampa who went by the stage name Dirty Redd.

Dirty Redd usually danced at Hollywood Nites and had to be the finest female from that area, or at least that's the way I felt about her fine, red sexy ass. She stood a mere five foot eleven with heels on and weighed around a hundred and fifty six pounds. Light skinned female with all of her curves in the right place. When she graced the stage, everybody in-side had their eyes all glued in on how spectacular she looked. You see Dirty Redd wasn't your average just any ole female trying to dance. She was the actual definition of a bad ass fucking female about to take your fucking money to see her perform. In other words, she made my girls and the rest of the girls inside that club that night look like amateurs in a big girl's world.

Meanwhile, as Disco stood on the stage introducing the ladies, O.J. and myself were standing off to the side smiling at one another because we knew what type of night we were both about to have.

One of our best ever, as the DJ had the room off the chain with some music playing from Cash Money Millionaires. The song was Bling, Bling.

As the song blasted from one end of the room to the other, the ladies were all rocking from side to side in their stilettos while I was standing there still smiling standing next to my brother who was looking like a fresh ass Kansas City Pimp.

"Boy you look like a hot mess!" I said to him while trying to maintain my cool and calm composure.

He just looked down at his outfit and then back up at me, while holding a small portion of the stash money in the air. "I'm that muthafuckin' nigga tonight. Who wants to dance for daddy?"

Chicken heads from all throughout the club started running up to him waving their hands as if he was about to throw money at them.

I quickly reached over and snatched up the money, as I shouted, "Man give me that fucking money before you buy up all the pussy in this muthafuckin' club!"

Chapter 14

Knee High Stockings!

Firstborn looked back at me with a shocked and stunned look on his face as he simply replied, "My bad, Baby Boy. I got carried away there for a minute."

"Yeah, that's what happens to niggas who go around bragging and boasting about how much money they have on them. They get taken away."

He still was looking confused as he asked. "What, they take them out of the club?"

"Nah fool, you become a marked man. You have to realize it's some thirsty ass niggas and bitches up in here. They spot someone with money and then follow their dumb ass back home and fucking rob them. Next thing you know is that you see their ass on the evening news."

"Oh yeah, I see what you're talking about now."

"Man whatever, keep checking on the girls while I go check on the room," I said to him as I walked away headed to the room to check on my surroundings.

While walking back to the Boom Boom Room, I had to stop and check my appearance in one of the full length mirrors that were aligned against the wall. Don't get me wrong, that night I was decked out in my new freshly tailored black Brooks Brother suit, with a silk white shirt along with a nice black and white striped tie to enhance. On my feet were a nice brand new pair of black and white Stacey Adams which were covering up a comfortable pair of black silk stockings.

That's right, a splendid pair of black silk women knee high stockings. Now for your brothers that don't know how to dress, the knee high stockings were an old trick I learned from one of my old Army buddies when I was stationed over in Hontheim, Germany.

The knee high stockings are what will enhance whatever you are wearing. You see the silk see through material gives your appearance that extra ultimate touch, not to mention the White Godfather hat I had sitting on top of my nice sexy sensual waves that adorned my scalp.

Sharon would always say to me. "Mike, if we have a boy, I want his hair to be just like yours."

Now that we were having a son, I hoped and prayed that he did come with a head full of good hair.

After stepping away from the mirror I peeked my head in to check on the Boom Boom Room to find everything in order. Just as I was about to turn around, Firstborn stepped behind me with.

"Yo, Baby Boy, the girls are all good and there is a line around the door of the club with people waiting to get in back here."

I looked back at him while giving him an evil grin.

"You know what that means right? Mo money, mo money."

"That's what I'm talking about!" he shouted while trying to dance. I guess no one ever told him that he couldn't dance a lick.

"Hey Firstborn, chill man, you over here acting like my homie, Aaron."

"You talking about that light skin pretty ass nigga who looks like Al B. Sure?"

"Yep," I said to him while laughing at the way he was trying to dance.

"Man, where is that cool ass nigga at anyway?"

"Back in Winter Haven, putting together a car lot."

"So, what, he's about to start up a car lot too?"

"Yep, and guess who he wants to run the business for him?"

"Who?" My brother asked as he held a dumbfounded look on his face.

"Me, that's who!"

"So, let me get this right, Baby Boy, you're going to give up all of this? The butt naked hoes and all the free pussy along with your nice ass house, so that you can move to Winter Haven, Florida to oversee a used car business?"

"Yep, one thing for certain and two things for sure my older unwise brother, this shit isn't promised forever," I replied to my brother as I walked away to check on the girls who were still in the center portion of the club on stage.

Chapter 15

Serious As A Heart Attack!

How wrong was I when it came to me ever leaving the Florida Hot Girls, who seemed to have some type of magical, mystical hold on me. As far as me leaving the Monster that I had created. You see the business of running one of the most elite, popular group of beautiful exotic women in Florida was not about to let me go. In other words, I was locked in for life, until death do us part as they say.

Meanwhile, the girls were coming down off of the stage as it was drawing closer for the festivities to start. Detective Protho and his good friend Detective Pass were seated off inside of their makeshift area that I had set up for them, with my ladies ready to start the show as they passed by me headed into the Boom Boom Room.

I calmly took the mic and walked to the center of the room and announced. "Without further ado, please put your hands together and get your money right. Ladies and gentlemen give it up two times for the world famous Florida Hot Girls!

The overcrowded room was going crazy as they started pulling females to their side of the room and began throwing money everywhere.

I was walking around with O.J. making change for the patrons when I looked over to my man and yelled, "Hey, it's so packed up in here that you're going to have to help me make change for some of the guys. Here is three stacks, tell the bar that you need more ones immediately!"

We had opened the door of the room around eleven thirty and it was already at capacity by twelve fifteen with a line of people still trying to get back inside of the room.

After I had sent O.J. to get more ones, my assistant stuck her head in the door and yelled out to me, "Michael, Michael!"

"Yeah," I replied trying to make my way to the door.

"Come here, please." Just as I had got back to the door she was yelling.

"Hey, the cash box is already full, you have to take this money so that I can put some more inside of it."

The poor girl had beads of sweat snaking down her fore head as she stood there in a panic.

"How much is in the box so far?"

She looked back at me, still sweating and in a frenzy.

"I don't know I didn't have time to count it."

"How many bands have you went through?"

"Hell, I don't know, maybe like six or seven."

"Okay, well it should be like six or seven thousand dollars inside the box."

After taking the money, I was back inside checking on my ladies and my two crooked ass friends. By now, they were pissy ass drunk I could tell by the way they were leaning while trying to maintain their balance inside of their chairs. Everything was going as planned when I heard the DJ playing the girls theme song by Cash Money I Need a Hot Girl.

Brothers started pulling their shirts off while trying to get naked right along with them bad ass Florida Hot Girls. Richard, who was standing next to me, was watching in awe when I leaned over to him and uttered. "Man, this place is about to be off the chain!"

He looked back at me looking like he had never seen that much ass and pussy in his young life and whispered, "I know man. Where is my girl, Chazz, because I need to smoke on some of that good good?"

I pointed to the rear of the club as I replied, "I think that she is over there in the corner of the back wall slow grinding on some brothers dick."

He immediately ran his weed head ass right over in the corner where she was, interrupting her while she was trying to make her money. I could hear her yell at him through the crowded room.

"Gone boy, I'll roll up another one after I finish my dance!"

He put his head down and turned back towards me and my brother.

"Damn, Baby Boy. That's lil cuz over there feening for a blunt like that?" Firstborn asked me while shaking his head in disbelief.

"Yeah man, now you see why your role plays a big part in whatever I do?"

"Yeah I see now. I'm glad that you made the right decision, or we might have had to take his ass out as well as the others!" Firstborn replied, while looking serious as a heart attack.

Chapter 16
Boys To Men!

With the crowd becoming larger than anticipated, it became closer for the execution of my final plan for my two dear friends. Besides, they were becoming too loud and obnoxious over in their corner, while throwing away all of their money. They were also drawing to much damn attention to themselves than what was needed. Firstborn had already been out to the limo twice to get more money for them to throw, due to Nicole and Entyce taking money from them throwing it to their girls, not to
mention the money that they were keeping for themselves as well.

Entyce had took like two racks, while Nicole had three, plus another five that she had took out of the brief
case while the two officers of the law were busy snorting some nose candy on the way to the club.

Those two cops were some real high rollers as they
were snorting powder, popping pills and going around fucking bitches raw. Rumor had it that both of them had extra kids on the streets from all of the unprotected sex they were having.

As I stood there observing them, it was plain and simple, they had to be stopped. There was no easy way out. They had to be disposed of immediately.

At first, I thought about putting their ass on a plane and sending them to Puerto Rico so that Sexy Redd could deal with them. But nah I had to cancel them before things got too far out of hand.

So I stood back for a second, still watching the girl's as they continued dancing for the crowded room of fans and females who wanted to be just like them. While standing there pondering on what to do, I was like should I throw their ass in a hotel room full of faggots and set them up or should I just have them erased from off the face of the earth.

If I set them up, they would have a chance to try and fight their case in the crooked court system and then somehow beat the charges, so we couldn't have that. Then there came the thought of having them being found some where dead. I could pin everything on them and be done with all of the trouble. No more questions and no more of them trying to extort me for more money. Their families would at least get a small fraction of their pension if I made it look like some type of drug deal gone bad. All I knew was that whatever I decided on, I would have to move fast. Time was ticking. By now, it was like two thirty in the morning and the club closed around three.

I was standing near the entrance of the club when Firstborn came up to me.

"Baby Boy, it's getting late what's the next move bro?" I heard him but I didn't answer right away, due to me being lost in thought.

"Baby Boy, what's up?" he asked again.

"Give me a minute," I replied as I snapped back to reality.

"Yeah, don't take too long;" Firstborn then looked down at his watch and then back at me while standing beside me chewing on a piece of spearmint gum. He made it look as if the gum he was chewing on was the last piece of gum on earth.

"Yeah, I gotcha," I replied as I walked away with my head down thinking of what to do next. Had those two cops did so much to me that I had to take their lives? Did they really deserved to die? I was standing there frozen stiff in thought when my conscience walked up dressed exactly like me.

'I thought you had the nerves to take another man's life.'

"I did too, but for some reason I'm having a change of heart."

'My young brother, should I remind you what is at stake if those two live through the night?'

"Nah, I understand fully. I just don't want to live with the aftermath of what happens next."

'Okay, I tell you what, Mister Scarry Ass Nigga. You take your black tailored made five hundred dollar suit wearing ass inside and tell them two cops that everything that they did today until right fucking now was a fucking lie! Then, tell them that you're not going to pay them one fucking dime of that two hundred fifty thousand dollars.

Then bring your pretty muthafucking ass back out here and tell me what the fuck they said!'

I looked at my conscience with a sad look on my face.

He looked back at me and recited, 'Listen here nigga, if your black ass goes down, I fucking go down right along with your black ass. I ain't going down for nobody and I sure as hell ain't going to prison. Look at us nigga, we ain't built for that type of life. Do you understand? So I tell you what we're going to do. We're going to put them two crooked ass niggas out of their misery this morning or sometime today. Now deal with that fuck nigga!'

I quietly asked my conscience. "Damn do you have to talk to me like that?"

'I got to do something before you get the both of us locked the fuck up for a very long time. I'm not about to be washing some niggas dirty ass boxers for some fucking Wham Whams nigga. I should've never let fucking Sexy Redd go back home!'

"And what do you mean by that?"

'Because when she was here, I didn't have to think for your black ass. She did. Now with her gone, it's like a part of you left with her! When she has our son, I hope that he's more like me than you!' I quickly stared back into his cold, dark brown eyes that looked like they were a deep black color at that moment.

"How do you know she's having a boy?"

'Because I make boys who become men.'

Chapter 17
Profitable Spots

While my conscience stood there belittling me, I couldn't help but hear this guy standing in front of me complaining to my assistant about one of the girls in the group.

"Listen lady, I really need to see the guy who runs these bitches!" he said in a loud aggressive tone to my assistant, who was trying to defuse the situation.

"Okay, what seems to be the problem young man?" My assistant asked him as politely as she could.

"Bitch, look at my gotdamn finger, One of them stank ass hoes inside that fucking room has something all over my damn index finger!" he shouted as he caught the attention of the people standing in line trying to still get in.

"Hold on, homeboy, I am not your bitch or anyone's else bitch, so could you please refrain from the disrespectful language?" she asked him, showing the utmost respect to the young rude gentleman.

"No, what is this white looking shit all over my finger?"

His finger looked like it had some cottage cheese all over it as she screamed.

"Ewwwww, what the hell is that foul looking stuff over your finger?"

"That's why I'm standing here asking to see Mike, or whoever the nigga is who's in charge of these nasty ass hoes!"

By now, I had had enough. I stepped in with, "Hold on homie, I've heard enough of what your trying to say. So what's really good?"

"You tell me. One of your females has this inside of her pussy." He then shoved his finger in my face.

"Hell, I don't know what that shit is, so why in the hell are you asking me?"

"Because one of your chicks is living foul, my nigga!"

I stood there trying to figure out what female he had stuck his finger in, when this lil ass nigga did the unthinkable. He turned around to the people standing in line and shouted out.

"Yo, look, y'all don't want to go inside this room. This want to be pimp ass nigga has a gang of dirty ass hoes up inside the club spreading shit like this all over a niggas fucking finger!"

Before I could even respond to what the brother had just said, my conscience sprang into action by grabbing the lil young ass brother with both hands up under his fat ass throat and pushed his ass up against the wall.

'Listen up, you lil short ass punk, Shut the fuck up before I beat the shit out of your ass and then make you suck that shit off of your fucking finger in front of everybody standing in line! Now, show me the female who you stuck your finger up in."

My conscience then took the lil nigga by his neck and took him inside of the room in which he pointed to this one lil slim, new chick that Lil Kitty had brought to the group that night.

I knew that this chick was going to be bad news when I met her Celie from the Color Purple looking ass. Honestly, she wasn't cut out to be a dancer, due to her being black as midnight, and having no shape at all. She had no ass; no titties and she was wearing some big ass glasses on her wide ass flat face. Not to mention the Cinderella looking outfit that she wore throughout the entire night that she was dancing. I made sure that I informed Lil Kitty that after that night she was not allowed to ever, ever, ever recruit anymore females for the group.

But little did I know that night was not only the night that she brought in a female that would give the girls a bad name. Them two chicks would be responsible for us losing one of our most profitable spots ever!

Chapter 18
Ms. Celie!

My conscience still had the lil nigga with the stank ass finger standing by the door, while he went to retrieve Ms. Celie from the back of the club. The unit that he held on his face said it all as he rapidly approached her. She had her back facing him as she stood there talking with her, best friend Lil Kitty.

Lil Kitty must've seen the look on his face as he was approaching. Her eyes grew bigger as she mumbled under her breath. "Shit, Mike is mad as fuck!"

Ms. Celie turned around to witness my conscience standing behind her, towering over her lil skinny body frame. He abruptly snatched her by her skinny ass arm and uttered, "Bring your black ass with me right now."

While he was dragging her ass out of the room. I could hear Lil Kitty saying to one of the other females. "Damn I wonder what she did to make him that fucking mad?"

When my conscience finally got her ass outside of the room, she was like. "What's wrong, Mike? What did I do?"

"Look at his fucking finger and please tell me what in the hell is that cottage cheese looking shit on his fucking finger?"

She looked at my conscience, then she looked over at the guy's finger, before looking over at my assistant who was standing there smiling back at her. Her lips began to quiver as she began to speak.
"You...see what had happened is that I had stopped by my boyfriend's house before I got here, and we had sex. I guess that must be his cum and my juices mixed up together all over his finger."

My conscience looked as if he wanted to explode as he angrily replied, "I be fucking damn. Didn't I tell you females to make sure that you all took care of your personal situations before you start dancing?"

She looked back at my conscience with those big ass bifocal glasses of hers as if she had just stole something.

"Yes Mike but I didn't think that it was still up inside of me," she replied as though she knew it was going to be her final night dancing with the Florida Hot Girls.

Meanwhile, the lil nigga with the fucked up ass finger had already run off to the bathroom to wipe his finger off, while my conscience was still standing their chewing Ms. Celie out. "I tell your ass what. Go back inside and tell Lil Kitty to come here, while you go ahead and dress back in. I'll call you when I need you to come back to work."

"Okay Mike," she uttered as she slowly walked away, since she knew it was her last night. My assistant who I guess felt sorry for her, cleared her throat and then muttered, "That dude was wrong for sticking his finger all up inside of her pussy though, Mike."

"Yeah, but those girls should always make sure that they have themselves clean before they start to dance. That lil nigga could have shut down the entire club. I don't know what that shit was that he had on his fucking finger."

While my assistant and I stood there discussing what had just transpired, Lil Kitty walked her lil narrow ass up, standing there with her hands on her lil ass hips, with her thong still being crooked all up in her lil thin ass.

"What, Mike?" she blurted out, while interrupting my assistant and me. "I was just about to make some more money before we shut down," she continued with before I could even reply, standing there smiling at me.

"Fuck that, you already shut down!" I shouted with a hand full of twenties.

"Why, who's shut down?" she asked as her smile disappeared from her elegant, cute ass face.

"Your lil ass. Now, go back inside and dress your lil short ass back in!"

"For what, Mike? It wasn't me with the funky ass pussy."

"I know it wasn't you, but you were the one who brought the girl with the funky ass pussy up in my spot to dance, with nut juice all up in here stank stank!"

Lil Kitty started laughing as she placed her hands on her knees trying to hold herself up from laughing so hard.

"Okay Mike, but listen I'm still making money up in here."

"Well, I guess you just stopped making money up in here, because you're dressing your lil short, crooked thong wearing ass back the fuck in."

"For what, it wasn't me with the fucked up pussy."

"Kitty, what time is it?"

She looked over at the clock on the wall and then uttered, "Oh, it's time to dress back in anyway."

"Yes Kitty."

My assistant and I then continued to count the money from the door as she went back inside to let the other girls know that it was time to dress in.

Chapter 19

Just as Lil Kitty had walked back into the crowded room of people in attendance, Firstborn emerged from behind the door and coolly whispered into my ear with.

"Yo, your two friends are inside about to pass out from being pissy ass drunk."

I calmly leaned back towards the as I murmured back.

"Wait until most of the crowd departs, then take them out through the side door and place them back inside of the limo."

"Word," he uttered as he eased back inside of the room, while my assistant and I stood there still counting up the loot.

"Excuse me," Chyna uttered as she stood behind us unnoticed.

"My bad, Chyna, how could I not see your cute ass standing there?"
"Whatever Mike, you still can't have any of this good ass pussy."

"Damn Chyna, that's how you feel?" I voiced with a shy grin across my face."

"Yes, are we going back to Jacksonville this weekend?" She asked as I stood up straight to answer her question.

"As of right now we are, why?"

"Because Mike, I really need to speak with those females who call themselves the Murder Queens.

"I turned my head and started counting my money again as I simply replied, "Well I don't know how you're going to do that, like I told you before I don't know who those females are."

"Mike, be for real. Even though I rode back with Richard on Sunday, I still heard what happened with you guys on the highway."

"And what was that Chyna?"

"That a couple of the girls who were riding back with you pulled out some fire and was going to take out some of the cops who had pulled you guys over!"

"Well, whoever told your yellow ass that must've lied to you, because we didn't have no damn shoot out with any cops, ole silly ass girl. Now, please take your beautiful ass back inside and dress back in!"

She began to walk away with a very distraught look on her face when she turned around and asked me.

"Hey Mike, how much is the tip out fee for tonight?"

"Let all the girls know that it's forty dollars."

"Okay."

As she walked away, I looked over to my assistant and mumbled.

"Hey, take this money and give to the manager of the club."

"How much is it?" She asked as she stepped away.

"About fifteen hundred. It's their cut for letting the girls dance here."

After she bent the corner, I stuffed the remaining bags of hard earned cash into my coat pockets and then stepped into the room with the females who were busy counting up their money.

Meanwhile, Firstborn had the limo pulled to the side of the building waiting on Nicole and Entyce along with their two drunk ass friends. I opened the side door of the club to watch as they all entered the limo, with my conscience stepping inside with them. Firstborn then slowly closed the rear passenger door and fleetly walked to the front of the limo. Just as the door closed, the rear passenger window lethargically came down as my conscience stuck his head out and winked his right eye at me. Then, he shouted out.

"Watch how the Murder Queens and I dispose of these two drunk ass officers of the law!" I dully closed the door with my head held down and whispered to myself.

"Damn I hope whatever they do to them brothers that it doesn't come back to bite me in my black ass later on down the road!"

Chapter 20
What In The Hell?

With the departure of those individuals that were about to do whatever it was they did, I calmly stood in the center of the room and asked.

"Okay, which one of you ladies have dates?" A few of them raised their hand as I instructed them to pay their fine for leaving the club with a guy to my assistant.

Once everything else was done, I walked O.J. and the splendid looking Sexy ass Dirty Redd to their car. Once they pulled off, I was on the way back inside to get the ladies so that we could all leave. Now this is where a beautiful relationship had to come to an end. It seemed as though after Wednesday night's show that Lil Kitty and her girl, Ms. Celie decided on getting a room at the Caribbean Beach Nightclub, which was a no no if you were about to do what they were about to do.

Those two bright individuals purchased one room and had like twenty people off inside of that one room. The hotel manager, who was also married to the owner of the club, found out about all the people they had in one room. In which the manager suspected that the two girls were inside the room prostituting all morning and wanted them out immediately.

Disco called me around ten thirty that morning and informed me that the club manager wanted to see me as soon as possible. I had only been asleep for a few hours when I got the call, so I quickly jumped up and took myself a shower. I then checked my time piece to see that it was around eleven twenty five.

After I got dressed, I went by Nicole's room to see if they had made it back in yet and to ask her how things had went with my two crooked friends. I slowly opened the door trying not to wake her as she quietly laid there fast asleep with some nice red silk panties covering up her beautiful pearl that laid off between her inner thighs.

I then gently closed the door so that I wouldn't wake her. I knew that if she was home, Entyce and Firstborn had to be home as well.

Now, even though I hadn't been asleep as long as seven hours, I was back on the road again about to handle some important business with the club owner and my man, Disco. My mind was running a mile a minute as I made a right turn onto Highway Fifty headed back to the club. At first, I was thinking to myself that maybe the club wanted to do another night or something with the Florida Hot Girls and I. Either way, I was just surprised to be going to see the club owner so fast. Whatever it was in my mind, it had to be good.

I never would have imagined in a million years that he was about to chop our heads off. While driving down Highway Fifty, I had on one of my slow CDs playing the song by Michel'le called Silly Love Song. I drifted back in forth day dreaming about Ms. Sharon and how I hadn't seen or heard from her lately.

It was only for a brief minute as my mind then thought of what had Firstborn and the girls did with Detective Protho and Pass. I sensed that he must have taken care of everything since he hadn't called me yet with any gory details of the event that took place.

As I pulled up into the parking lot of the club, the owner was standing there at the door waiting on me with a scowl on his tall Arabian looking face.

"What's good, fellows?" I asked him as Disco emerged from another door sipping on something to wake him up.

The manager then greeted me before whisking me off to the room where Lil Kitty and her group had stayed that early morning. While walking towards the room, I glanced over at Disco. "Pss, hey man, what in the hell is going on?"

Disco looked back over at me. "You're about to find out."

"Damn, that serious huh? What, somebodies dead back here or something?"

He then looked over at me while replying, "Yeah, you and them hoes, my man!"

I quickly snapped back with. "What?"

We all had just got to room one twenty one as the manager knocked on the door. There was no answer at first, so he then began bamming on the door as if he was the police.

"What in the hell is going on?" I asked Disco again. This time he just put his head down without even making eye contact with me.

Chapter 21

After The Club!

By now, I knew that something had to be wrong, because Disco wasn't smiling like he usually did. After about five minutes of the owner knocking and beating on the door, Lil Kitty sluggishly opened the door and didn't even bother to see who it was knocking and trying to beat the door down. She had nothing on but the thong that always seemed to be crooked hanging in her ass along with a cut off T-shirt that was showing off her nice lil perky titties, which were nestled up on her small chest ready for someone to suck them as if they were a newborn baby.

As she walked, her lil tight booty ass back over to the bed in which she briskly jumped back into.

When the manager pushed the door back, I was like, "Damn, where did all those muthafuckers sleep at?" It was like ten to fifteen people scattered out over the bed and floor, women and men. It was like a bunch of Mexican's all over that small ass hotel room. People were all passed out with different people's underwear sprawled out over the floor. It was like they had a big ass orgy up in that room, which smelled like corn chips and ass.

The owner was furious. It wasn't the fact that she had purchased a room. He was mad at the fact that the lil shorty had purchased only one room for all those people. And we all know how them people get when you try to cheat them out of their hotel money. And to add gas to the fire, he was highly upset that he had us working in his club and that he was only charging us thirty five dollars a night for a room.

The owner then turned to me while the three of us stood there looking at all the people laying there on the floor and bed still sleep. "I want her and all of these people out of my establishment right now and there will be no more Florida Hot Girls dancing at my Club! You and the Florida Hot

Girls are done here!" Him and Disco turned and walked away while leaving me there to give Lil Kitty the bad news.

I walked into the room trying not to step on anyone laying there on the floor as Lil Kitty stood up to hear me say. "Thanks, Lil Kitty, the Florida Hot Girls have just been fired from dancing here at the Caribbean. So, please get dressed. The manager wants you guys out of here ASAP!"

She was rubbing the crust from her eyes and looking for her clothes before the cops arrived when she asked me.

"Mike, do you think if I go in there and apologize that he might change his mind and let us keep dancing here?" I kept my head, trying not to be angry at her, still boiling over the fact that we had just lost the most lucrative spot ever.

I looked down at her and replied, "Nah Kitty, it's over baby. I'll just see you tomorrow, talk at cha later." I then kissed her on the cheek and turned headed for my car, as I looked back at what once was one our most profitable night spots.

Now it was all thrown away because of one lil narrow ass female and Ms. Celie from the Color Purple who wanted to get their freak on after the club.

Chapter 22
The Door!

As I drove to the entrance of the parking lot, I stopped to look left making sure that there was no oncoming traffic before pulling out into the highway. Once I saw that the coast was clear I made a right turn headed towards the intersection up ahead. Just as I got to the intersection, I made a left turn onto Kirkman Road headed towards Metro West, thinking to myself of how I couldn't wait to get back home, away from everybody and everything that was troubling me.

As I slowly crept down Kirkman Road I placed me head against my window, lost in thought, still stewing over the fact that we had just lost one of our most lucrative spots to date. What would we do now to accommodate the loss? I would be lying if I said that I didn't care about losing that spot. Not only was it a nice payday for me whenever we worked that club, but it was a nice payday for my girls as well.

When I finally made it back home, I didn't notice the grey sedan parked off to the right of my house. I dully sat there still lost in thought inside of my car, when I was suddenly startled by a tap at my window. I abruptly looked up to witness two white detectives, standing there at my window with what looked like snarls on their beat red face. "Fuck, what in the hell did they want? I sure as hell hope it's not for the three warrants that I have on my ass," I said under my breath as I slowly let down the window.

"Good day, Mr. Vallentino, you're a very hard man to keep up with, sir. May we have a word with you?" the one tall, slim white officer asked as he cut a wicked half grin at me.

"Yes, could we make this brief as possible. I had a very long night and I'm still somewhat sleepy," I replied as I stepped out of my car with a fucked up expression on my face.

As I stood there listening to the lead officer, I happened to look up and see that my bedroom curtains were slightly open. I stood there in a daze at the shadow or person who was staring down at us through my bedroom window, thinking to myself of who could be in my bedroom.

"So Mr. Vallentino, you say that you have no idea what happened to the officers that were seen out last night with you and your female employees?"

"That's correct, sir. Like I just stated to you, I have no idea what or where they went after leaving the club?"

"Well, if you do happen to see or him from them anytime soon, will you give us a call when you do."

I slowly took the card that the officer held out for me to take and replied, "Yes officers, I'll be in touch with you two if I hear anything or find anything out about the two missing officers."

Just as I had taken the card from his hand, he said. "Thank you once again, sir. Make sure that you get some rest."

"Thank you, detective and you do the same. I wouldn't want whatever happened to you partners to happen to you two officers as well."

The one officer in the back hastily turned around. "What was that Mr. Vallentino?"

"Oh nothing sir, I was just saying that I would hate for something bad to have happened to your two detectives. That's all, sir.

He began to turn around as he uttered, "Yeah, for a minute there I could have sworn that you actually knew something that we didn't."

I stood there smiling as the two detectives got into their grey police issued sedan and drove away. I watched as the car bent a right out of the complex, then I looked back upstairs to see my curtains abruptly close. That's when I dashed for the front door headed straight for my bedroom, hoping to find the person still there. I was running so fast that I was leaping the stairs at least three at a time, hoping to catch the culprit. Just as I reached the top of my stairs I lunged for my bedroom door and quickly opened the door.

Chapter 23

Wanted Dead!

I could sense that someone or something evil had been in my bedroom watching me and the officers, while we stood downstairs talking in my driveway. I numbly searched the room with my eyes when I caught him standing there smiling at me the same way he was smiling the night before when he left with the girls and my brother.

Once we made eye contact, he grayly walked over to where my big screen television was and turned it on. He then turned to me and said.

"So what did they want?"

"You know what they wanted. They wanted to know about their partners."

"That's it. Well there isn't a need for you to worry yourself about those two. Firstborn and I, along with those two cute Murder Queens, disposed of those two earlier this morning!"

I put my head down as I sat on my bed, feeling sorry for what had to be done. "So, what did you all do them?" I asked still feeling remorseful for my actions.

My conscience then turned the television to Channel Nine and stepped back while looking at me with a devilish grin on his face. "It makes no difference now, they're both in a better place. And with them two gone, we both can sleep better now." I sat there with my head resting in the sweaty palms of my hand and then lifted my head to say.

"Damn, do you have to be so damn cold about what-ever it is you all did?"

He angrily stepped in front of me with anger in his cold, malice looking eyes and sputtered, "Cold, nigga stop acting as if you didn't do your part in having them two clowns killed. Here, look at what the news people have to say about what happened!"

"What in the hell have you done?" I asked him as he stood there growling at me as if he was a ferocious pit bull ready to attack. While standing there with the same exact suit I had on the night before.

"You mean what have you done now? You see every time that I do, you do as well. For the last time, we're both the same exact person, Michael Vallentino. Don't you forget that. Now watch the television screen as they report on how gruesome they found those two crooked ass detectives that you wanted dead!"

Chapter 24
Violent Side!

The television screen lit up as if he had given it a cue to turn on. When it did, there sat the glamorous news anchor, Latasha Willis. I froze as her lips parted and she began to recite.

"This is Latasha Willis with Channel Nine breaking news. Two Bridgeville homicide detectives have been found shot to death at the old industrial warehouse off of Highway Ninety-eight and Hubert Hurst Road. Camelia Fields is there on location. Camelia could you tell us what happened?"

"Yes Latasha, it seems as though these two highly decorated officers where involved with some type of undercover drug and money loitering scheme in which it all came to abrupt halt earlier this morning here at this industrial site. Where, only a few weeks ago, the bodies of several known drug dealers and prostitutes were also found badly burned in this same area. The names of the two deceased homicide detectives are Detective Tyrone Protho, who had been on the force since leaving the military back in 1990. His partner of fifteen years, Marty Pass was the other detective who met his untimely death earlier this morning. He too had been a member of the Armed Forces as well as his partner. Sources here close to this case believe now that these same two officers may have been responsible for the death of those individuals found here only weeks ago. As this story unfolds I will bring you more up to date information as we obtain more news about this horrific crime scene. This has been Camelia Fields reporting for Channel Nine News, back to you Latasha."

"Thank you, Camelia. Trevor Jones, the police chief will give a live statement about this crime in about four hours, so please stay tuned to Channel Nine News for more up to date info as Channel Nine was first to bring you this story."

My conscience slowly turned to me with that evil grin of his as I stood there with my mouth wide open as to what I had just witnessed. He held that menacing grin on his face and then uttered, "Answer your phone, it's your lil boo thang calling."

I looked back at him and replied, "My phone isn't ringing!"

As soon as I said that to him, my phone started ringing. I pulled my phone from my pocket and looked to see that it was Sharon calling.

"Hello." I answered still in shock.

"Baby, where are you?" Her voice rattled, sounding nervous in the background of the phone speaker.

"I'm home baby, why, what's wrong?" I said back to her as my conscience stood there looking out of the window, still dressed in black.

"Did you see the news?" She asked me as I could hear the cracking in her voice.

"Yes I did, it's crazy, isn't it?"

"Yes, it is, Michael and what seems to be outrageous is that those two crooked ass cops are responsible for the death of my cousin and probably the disappearance on my fucking uncle! Bae, those were the same two cops who came by your apartment and my house acting like they were really concerned about what was going on. Can you believe this shit?" She asked me while talking a mile a minute.

"Bae, I know I saw everything on the news. Are you going to be alright?"

"I'm fine. I just cannot believe how those two officers have been going around here fooling everybody, while all along they were the culprits to the damn thing."

"Yeah, I know right," I replied as I sat down.

"Are you busy right now Michael?"

"Nah, not really. Why, what's up?"

"I'm on my way to your house, is that okay with you?"

Just as she had asked me that, my conscience suddenly turned around to me while frantically shaking his head at me. "No, no, no!" He was saying as I replied to Sharon.

"Yeah bae, come on over. I'll be here waiting on you," I said to her while my conscience for the first time seemed like he was the one nervous now.

"I love you Michael."

"Love you too, Sharon." I replied as I hung up the phone, only to hear my conscience scream.

"Man are you fucking crazy, it's still some things that we have to cover up before anyone else can come over here!" He yelled while displaying his violent side.

Chapter 25
Even There!

I stood there feeling as if I was missing something, when I asked my conscience.

"Okay and what's that Mister I Have Everything Under Control!"

He looked back at me confused and somewhat agitated when he mumbled. "Mike, it's entirely too early for us to allow anyone here. This very house that we live in is a horrific crime scene!"

"What are you talking about?" I asked him as I stood there looking out of the window, with my hands stuffed inside of my pants pocket.

"The limo that has parts of those two officers' brains inside of it is downstairs in the garage at this very moment!" He blurted out in anger and frustration.

"What?" I screamed in sheer astonishment at what he had just said to me.

"I said that the limo that we used to dispose of those two officers is downstairs with parts of their brain splattered all inside of it!"

Just as he had finished his sentence, I was running full speed downstairs to the garage, not knowing what to expect when I got there.

Upon opening the door, I found Firstborn sweating from the heat as he was busy cleaning out the limo. I shouted out his name as I saw him about to bend over and start vacuuming out the limo.

"Firstborn!" he lifted his head up from the back of the limo with a Black and Mild hanging from his dry, crust-stained lips, looking at me as if I knew what he was doing with the limo.

"Yeah, what's up with cha, Baby Boy?"

"Why is the limo that you guys used last night back here at my damn house?" I asked him with shock and disgust in my voice, due to seeing that damn limo back at my house.

But before he could answer my question, Nicole and Entyce were running their half-naked bodies downstairs.

"Michael!" Nicole shouted at me while standing behind me in some Apple Bottom shorts along with a wife beater T-shirt that was to small trying to cover up her nice, beautiful breasts.

"What is it, Nicole? Don't you see that I'm trying to talk with my brother?" I yelled back in her direction.

"That's why I'm here. It's because of us that the limo is here at the house!" Nicole said to me while standing there with the lips of her vagina hanging to one side of her Apple Bottom shorts.

"What?"

She began to tremble as she recited. "On the way to the industrial site earlier this morning, the one detective named Pass wanted to eat my pussy. We thought that the spiked alcohol would have knocked the both of them out by the time that we left the club, but his ass was still somewhat awake as he laid his round headed ass between my legs."

"Okay, get to the point Nicole as to why this damn limo is parked in my garage, with Firstborn cleaning it out!"

"He saw the tattoo and was like Murder Queens. That's when he jumped back as if he was about to reach for his police issued revolver. Before I knew it, I had pulled out my four nickel and took off the front of his quite large forehead," she said as tears began to snake down her beautiful face.

"Damn, what about Detective Protho?" I asked her as I pulled her closer to me, so that I could place my arms around her quivering body.

"Well, that's when his partner, Detective Protho jumped up trying to retrieve his weapon not noticing me sitting behind his ass. I quickly pulled out my 9 mm that I had tucked away behind the console and shot him in the back of that little pill head of his. It caused all of his brains to splash all over the backseat, in which your dear brother here is cleaning up right now," Entyce said to me as I stood there still holding onto a nervous and frightened Nicole.

"So, you guys botched up the whole entire plan I see," I replied with a sour expression covering my face.

"Nah, baby brother, that's when you jumped in with the coldest plan ever! I know that you have seen the news this morning. You have that whole entire industrial site look-ing like a damn drug deal gone bad. But what's funny is that you were acting as if you were out of it the whole entire time. Like we weren't even there!"

Chapter 26

Sinister Smile!

I stood there listening and watching Firstborn explain this morning events as he blew out billows of smoke from his Black and Mild. I cut him off mid-sentence when I uttered, "Whatever. How long is it going to take you to clean out this damn limo?"

He smiled as usual and then replied, "At least another three hours. I got this; you just handle everything else." I turned to walk away as I still had Nicole in my grasp. She looked up at me while looking so inviting in her Apple Bottom shorts, with her phat, stupid, red butt hanging out of them.

"Mike, you're not mad at us are you?"

"No, Nicole I just thought that since you guys were the professionals that you all would have handled things a lot better than you all did."

"We did, Mike. It's just that when Detective Pass saw the Murder Queens tattoo something must've snapped inside of his head," Entyce emitted as she stood there in the kitchen foyer, trying to hide her beautiful breast inside of her Victoria Secret black silk see through attire.

"Yeah and that's when I pulled out that four nickel without thinking twice from out of the crack of that seat and blew that niggas cap straight off. You should've seen the look on that niggas face as the top of his head flew off before he succumbed to his awful demise!" Nicole voiced as she poured her something to drink.

"Like your brother said though Mike, if it wasn't for your quick thinking, we all would probably be in the county jail right about now," Entyce said as she walked over to the kitchen window to witness Mignon and Strawberry outside by the pool area chilling.

"Okay, enough already of what happened this morning. Sharon should be here any minute you guys go ahead and put on some clothes while I get ready for her arrival.

"Is she going to be here long, because I do want to spend some quality time in your arms today?"

"I really don't know right now, Nicole. I do know that she wants to probably talk about her cousin's funeral this Saturday."

"Oh, I had forgot all about that. Do we have to attend?"

"You guys have a Bachelor Party this Saturday night in Jasper, Florida. So, if you guys don't want to go, that's fine. I'll just leave after the funeral and meet you guys in Jacksonville."

"Thanks, Mike. Well enjoy your company I'll see you later," Nicole said as she walked upstairs with her ass swaying from side to side.

Minutes later, Sharon was ringing the doorbell. I opened the door just as she was stepping back off of the concrete doorstep that adorned the entrance of the huge estate that we called home.

"Hello boo," I said to her, standing there with a Kool-Aid smile across my face.

She came through the door of the house with. "Damn Michael, what took you so long to answer the door? Were you in here hunching?"

"Hunching? Damn Sharon, I haven't heard that term since middle school. And no I was upstairs," I replied as she stood on her tippy toes to place a kiss on my lips.

"So, are you okay?" I asked her as soon as we had finished kissing.

"Yes, now that we all know who killed my cousin and maybe my uncle, who no one seems to be able to locate," she replied as she began to walk upstairs to my room.

"Did you see the news bulletin at one this afternoon?"

"No, why was there more to see, because I turned it off as soon as it was over," I replied to her question.

"Yes, it seems like those two crooked individuals were involved with a lot more than just the average day to day police business at hand. Them two cops had two brand new houses out here in Metro West that they had just purchased along with two brand new Mercedes Benz and on top it off, they said that they had stolen like two hundred and fifty thousand dollars from the police department. The police even said that they confiscated some paperwork showing where they were about to leave the country on an around the world vacation."

"Damn Sharon, they said all that about them boys?" I asked her as I closed the door to my bedroom, while displaying a sinister smile.

Chapter 27
Another Child!

Sharon sat her lovely, nice sized hips onto my bed as she replied, "I guess so baby. All I know is that my family really needs to be compensated, since those cops were the ones responsible for her death."

"I can agree with you on that, beautiful. Now, how is everything else looking for the funeral this Saturday?"

I guess everything is fine. My mother says that some more of the family members are coming down this Friday. Are you still going to be able to attend the funeral with me?"

"Yes, baby, I wouldn't want you to go by yourself. Besides, I know you need me there for moral support." She smiled at me as she shouted. "Shut up Mike. The baby, and I are starving. Where are you taking us for lunch?"

I looked down at my time piece to see that the time was two thirty. That's when I looked up at her still sitting there on the bed with her legs crossed. "Well, it's like two thirty and lunch time is over. Since I know that you love Red Lobster so much, why don't we just head there."

She jumped off the bed, smiling as she shouted. "Yes, and I can't wait to order me some lobster tails along with some crab legs!"

Okay Sharon let's go. I would hate for the baby and you to starve on my behalf," I said to her as I grabbed my money clip from off of the dresser and placed it inside of my pants pocket.

The both of us had just got downstairs. I knew that Firstborn was still inside the garage cleaning the limo so I couldn't open it to take one of the other vehicles. So we took the Q-45 that was still parked outside of the garage.

As I was opening the door for Sharon to get inside, Firstborn decided that he had to open the damn garage door.

I looked back as the door was going up saying to myself. "Oh no, please don't let that damn limo still be full of those officers' blood and brains!" The door had just went up when we both met eye to eye.

Sharon seen the expression on my face as she asked. "Hey baby, why does the man inside your garage look a bit like you?"

I was stunned for a minute until I realized that she hadn't met my brother yet.

"Oh Sharon, I'm so sorry. Meet my brother, James Firstborn Vallentino, the third. Firstborn, meet Sharon Conoly."

His giant smile beamed off of his wide as face as he lingeringly approached the vehicle. "Hello beautiful, nice to meet you. My brother here has told me so much about you," Firstborn said as he extended his hand out to Sharon.

"The pleasure is all mine young man. I hope Mike here hasn't told you anything bad about me?" she said as he took her small hand into the palm of his hand and kissed the top of her hand.

"No I must say, it's been all good my fair lady. One thing for sure is that he didn't say that you were as beautiful as you are."

"Stop it, I say. Mike if I didn't know any better, I would say that you get your charm from your brother."

"Whatever Sharon, you have it all wrong. He gets his charm from me. Everything else he gets from our father," I said as he just stood there smiling and trying to look between her legs.

I gave him a quick nudge before asking him. "Yo Firstborn, we're about to grab a bite to eat. Do you want me to pick you up something?"

"Nah, Baby Boy I'm good. I want to finish this up before it gets too late."

"Alright bro, I'll see you when we get back."

"Peace," Firstborn said to me as I was pulling out of the driveway.

While driving away from the house, I could see Nicole standing in the kitchen window with a unit on her face. It had got to the point where is Nicole wanted more of my time and whenever Sharon was around, she didn't like it one bit. She knew that Sharon was expecting our first child together and it seemed as if she wanted to carry one of my children as well. Whatever it was that she wanted I knew for a fact that I didn't want any part of it.

Every day that I had to see her, I began to regret the moment of ever having unprotected sex with her. Especially with the comment she had made only a few days prior. I was sure that she was trying to trap me into being the father of another child.

Chapter 28
Pregnant Too!

After Nicole watched us drive away, she dingily walked back upstairs with attitude and just a tad bit of jealousy in her heart. You could actually see the smoke coming from her nostrils as she angrily pushed her bedroom door open. Once inside of her space, it was there that she began to devise of a sure plan to get rid of her competition. Her beautiful face held a disarming smile as she sat there lost in thought with what she had or what she was planning for my precious Sharon, it wasn't until Mignon burst into her bedroom with.

"Hey, you busy?" Mignon asked her as she waltzed into her room, with a towel wrapped around her elegant looking body.

"Nah chick, just sitting here thinking. Why what's up wit cha?" Nicole asked her as she snapped back from the dark place inside of her devious sinister little mind. "Nothing, just wondering why you're in here and not outside with us at the pool, enjoying all of this beautiful Florida sunshine."

"I would be chick, but I'm in here with something on my mind."

"There you go, what's wrong now?" Mignon asked as she sat down next to Nicole, placing her arm around her shoulders.

Nicole shrugged her arms away as she stood up placing her foot hard onto the carpet floor before answering Mignon back with, "Girl I'm so tired of Michael's lil boo thang," she said as she walked over to her bedroom window.

"Nicole, what are you talking about now, girl?"

"Sharon girl!" Nicole blurted out as she angrily turned to face Mignon.

"What about her?"

"Mike and her lil red ass just left, headed for Red Lobster. This lil heifer always comes over here and gets her way with my damn man and I have just about had enough of it!" Nicole shouted as she folded her arms and placed them over her nice, tight petite stomach.

Mignon cut a devious smile on her face as she recited to Nicole. "The way I see things is that Mister Mike here is everybody's damn man."

"Whatever, Mignon. If Sharon keeps getting in my way and between my emotions, she might just have to meet the chick who doesn't mind getting rid of another bitch in order to keep what's hers!"

Mignon jumped up off of the bed in disbelief as she ran over to Nicole. She snatched her by her arm before uttering, "Damn, bitch, you serious as a heart attack about that nigga, huh?"

"You damn skippy bitch," Nicole replied as she looked in the eyes of Mignon with fire.

"Well, whatever you decide to do, please don't include my lil red ass in it, Nicole."

"Don't worry, won't nobody know but me and my baby," Nicole replied as she began to walk out of her room.

Mignon was right behind her with a shocked look on her face as she shouted out, "Nicole, Nicole, girl please don't tell me that your pregnant too?"

"Talk to you later, Mignon," Nicole voiced as she walked out of her room headed back downstairs, with Mignon standing at the top of the stairs screaming. "Nicole, Nicole, Nicole, girl bring your lil crazy ass back here!"

Chapter 29
Dents In His Head!

At 10:35AM Friday morning I woke up next to Sharon laying there next to me fast asleep, like she had been at someone's job the previous night before, working all night long. Funny thing about that was that Sharon didn't have a job. Now with me pinning her cousins murder on those two crooked cops, she was about to find out that neither her nor her family would ever have to work another day in their life again.

The time was now around 10:55 am as I laid there staring up at the ceiling pondering the last few hours of my complicated life through my mind.

First, it was the thought of the two detectives being murdered in the unpleasant way that they were. Then, it was the constant thought of me taking the life of Sharon's cousin Do- Dirty, which was the mother to Richard's two beautiful young daughters. Finally, it was the perpetual thought of what Sharon's cousin, Tamika had said to me only a few days ago. Something about a daughter that I might have fathered along with her, years ago.

My head was spinning as I laid there with all of that on my mind. What was I going to do next? Do-Dirty's funeral was the next day as I mumbled to myself while trying to slide out of bed without disturbing Sharon from out of her deep sleep. I was actually dreading the thought of having to attend her funeral, knowing that I was the one responsible for her death.

Just as I was about to escape from the grasp of Sharon's arm, her phone began to erupt. I was too late as the phone woke her up suddenly from her deep sleep on the fourth ring. She clumsily knocked the phone off of the nightstand as she fumbled around to retrieve it.

"Shit, this damn phone gets on my last nerves," she said as she rolled out of bed half-naked trying to answer it. She finally reached it before it stopped ringing with half of my silk bed sheets wrapped around her majestic looking half naked body. "Hello," she said sounding all groggy. "Yes ma'am, this is her," she mumbled as I was still laying there trying to pretend that I was still sleep while lying there trying to eavesdrop on her conversation with whomever it was that she was on the phone with. "Okay ma'am, we shall be there within a few hours, thank you." Sharon then hung up the phone as I could see her out the corner of my eyes looking over at me with those cute hazel brown eyes of hers.

"Michael, Michael, wake up!"

I rotated over smiling at her while stretching my arms yawning at the same time.

"What's up boo?" I said to her as I stood up to look out of my bedroom window, trying to see how nice the day was at that time of the morning.

"Michael, that was some lady from the police department named Mrs. Dunbar."

"Okay and what does Mrs. Dunbar have to do with me this morning, beautiful?" I said to her while turning around to see her sitting up in my bed with seven hundred and fifty dollars of my silk sheets wrapped around her beautiful naked body that looked even more inviting by her being impregnated with my child.

"Nothing silly ass man. They need my aunt and mother, along with me down at the department around 2:00 this afternoon."

"For what?" I asked her as I walked towards the bathroom.

"I don't know. She said that she would explain everything to us when we all got down there.

"Okay, well I guess that means that you all are about to get paid."

"Whatever, Michael. I need to get in the shower before I get dressed. Are you coming down to the station with us?"

"Nah I think that I'm going to lay around here for a few more hours. I'm still tired from what you did to me last night."

"Whatever Michael, with the way that you were all up in me last night I hope that you wasn't hitting my baby in his head with that long ass dick of yours."

"Girl, stop playing and get your lil fine ass in the shower. You know good damn well that you can't hit no baby in the head with no dick."

"Yes, you can Michael. Remember the other day when everybody was at my house?"

"Yeah, and?"

"Well, the lil boy who was there named Raynard has dents in his head, due to his father making love to his mother so damn hard and trying to hit the bottom when she was carrying lil Raynard. Even my cousin P Jay from Gainesville said that she knew this one chick who baby daddy was hitting her the same way that it put dents in her sons head as well."

Chapter 30
Huckle Buck!

I came out of the bathroom just after brushing my teeth, when I looked at Sharon laughing and uttered. "Sharon, that is the craziest, country ass story that I have ever heard." I had just got back into the bedroom when she walked by me smiling with all of her fine ass body of hers tucked away in her towel. She then intentionally dropped the towel from around her so that I could see how fine she was.

"Damn, your ass is getting so damn phat. Let me see if I can touch our baby's head from the back," I said to her as I followed her into the bathroom.

"Whatever, Michael."

A few minutes later, I was making love to her as she stood there on her tip toes inside of the shower. She slowly turned around to me as I gently went up in inside of her soaking wet vagina.

"Damn Mike I've never been in this position before."

"I know, just wait. You haven't seen nothing yet. I have another position that you haven't been in yet neither."

"And what position is that?" she asked as she reached for the tiled wall before she began thrusting back and forth, moving her body in sync with me.

" I have to wait until you have the baby, the position is called the Huckle Buck."

The what, Michael?" she asked as she burst out into laughter with the mention of the name of the position in question.

"The Huckle Buck," I answered as I continued pounding her fine red ass, as she tried to keep her composure after reaching her third orgasm.

"Whatever Michael."

"Chill, Sharon. I'll demonstrate it to you later but for now just keep down all the screaming so that we both can enjoy the moment."

Meanwhile, there was a knock at the bedroom door of Mignon.

"Come in," Mignon said to whomever it was knocking at her door.

"Hey, you still sleep?" The person asked as they slowly pushed the door open.

"Nah, how could I with all of the commotion that Michael and Sharon are making in his room," Mignon said to Strawberry as she sat on the edge of Mignon's king size bed, that was covered with some nice white Persian silk bed sheets that Mignon said cost somewhere in the neighborhood of two thousand dollars.

"Girl, you are not going to believe what Nicole said to me last night," Strawberry said to Mignon, who was now sitting up in her bed listening to the words coming out of Strawberry's mouth.

"Well, it can't be no worse than what she said to me when Michael and Sharon left for Red Lobster yesterday. The lil bitch has lost her damn mind if you ask me Strawberry. I actually think that she's going to do something drastic to Nicole."

"She said the same thing to me as though she wants me to help her with her evil ass plan," Strawberry said to Mignon, who had just pulled her sheets back revealing her nice looking camel toe that was staring directly at Strawberry, who we know had her beady lil ass eyes plastered on the beautiful sight staring her right dab smack in the face.

"Man, the lil heifer is really tripping, talking about showing Sharon how the Murder Queens get down."

"Nah, Mignon," Strawberry replied as her dick sucking lips fell to the floor.

"Yes, Strawberry. I told her lil short ass not to get me involved in whatever it was she was thinking about doing."

"I know that's right," Strawberry replied as she still kept her eyes glued on Mignon's camel toe.

"She was like no one was going to know but her and her newborn baby."

"Shut up girl, you telling me that Nicole is pregnant too?"

"Yes child, at least that's what she was trying to tell me yesterday."

"Does Mike know, Mignon?"

"I have no idea, Strawberry. All I know is what she told me yesterday."

Chapter 31

Buy This One!

Mignon was walking towards her shower when she turned around and replied, "Man, when Mike finds out, shit is really going to hit the fan."

"Well, I ain't got shit to do with it. I just hope that whatever happens, doesn't fuck up what we have with the group," Strawberry replied as she stared at how Mignon waltzed her lovely thick, juicy ass past her.

Strawberry was stuck with the thought of how nice Mignon's pussy would taste in between her lips while sitting there on the edge of Mignon's bed not seeing anything but the nice ass that was stuck on Mignons back, when Mignon said, "Hey, let me get a quick shower so that we all can go do some shopping to help ease the tension, that we all have on our mind." Strawberry snapped out of her narcosis state of mind and then quickly uttered. "Do we take Nicole with us?"

"If you want to ask her crazy ass, that's up to you."

"Alright, I'll check with her. In the meantime, I should be ready in about two hours."

"Gotcha, Strawberry," Mignon replied as she closed the door to her bathroom and then jumped into the hot, steamy pulsating shower.

Meanwhile, it was around twelve thirty, midafternoon when I walked Sharon to her car and then stood there watching her drive away all excited about her family getting some needed support from the death of her cousin. I had just entered back into the house when Firstborn came from around the corner of the kitchen, yelling.

"Good morning, Baby Boy."

I shrugged my shoulders as I gave him a dumbfounded look and replied, "It's after twelve noon, Firstborn. So it's good afternoon to you."

"My bad, Baby Boy. Hey, about yesterday. I didn't know that you had your girl Sharon out front with you when I opened the garage."

"No problem, Firstborn, just next time be more mind full of your surroundings. Not only was Sharon out front, but the cops had rolled up on me earlier that morning. The entire time that I was out front talking with them I had no idea that you were in the garage cleaning out the limo."

"What, you mean to tell me that it was some cops out front talking with you, and I was inside with portions of those cops brain splattered everywhere?" he replied looking surprised and shocked, at what I had just told him.

"Yep and it's a good thing that the blood from them two cops didn't run out of the limo down the driveway."

"You're absolutely right, Baby Boy. Damn, I didn't think about that. I really messed up, didn't I?" he asked as I stood back staring at him while leaned up against the kitchen sink.

"Almost Firstborn, that's why I have to think for you and everybody else around here."

He looked like he was sincere about his mistake, when he said the smartest thing I think I ever heard him say. "Well, I might as well let you know this now, before it's too late."

"Oh shit, what is it now?" I said as I stood there with disgust written all over my face.

"It would be best if we pull out the seats in the back of the limo and put new ones back there."

"Why?" I asked while standing there looking back at him as if he knew something that I didn't.

He then looked me directly in the eyes and said, "Just to make sure that we or should I say me, don't leave any brain fragments that I might have missed in between the seats," he replied.

For the first time he made sense, that's when I replied, "Sounds good to me. Do what you have to do so that we don't run into any problems down the road."

"Alright, Baby Boy, I'll get at cha after all of this is done."

"Okay, I guess I might as well go ahead and call Preston over at Prestige Limo Service and ask him how much this particular limo cost. Because it looks like I'm going to have to buy this one!"

"Yep, you might as well do that Baby Boy, because it damn sure looks that way," Firstborn replied as he walked away to take the seats out of the limo.

Chapter 32

Versace Shades.

While that was taking place at my house, there was something more sinister and gruesome happening down at the police station. Something so gruesome that the person who found it, had to call someone higher on the food chain in his department.

One of the Lab Technicians, who was working on the bodies of Detective Protho and Detective Pass had made a hideous discovery. One that caused him to call the immediate supervisor of the two dead homicide detectives.

The office phone rang two times when the Lt. answered. "Hello, Lt. Richards speaking."

The young lab tech was a tad bit nervous as he spoke back into the receiver with. "Yes, this is officer Charles here at the forensic lab. Do you have a brief minute, sir?"

"Yes, what can I do for you officer?"

The lab tech paused for a short minute before answering. "We seem to have ourselves a bit of a problem Lt. Richards."

Lt. Richards leaned forward into his desk and frowned as he replied, "And what might that problem be young man? What was your name again son?"

"Officer Charles, sir."

"Okay son, now what is the problem Officer Charles?"

"The two homicide detectives that were killed at the warehouse the other day."

"Yes, what about them?"

"It seems as though sir they weren't killed at the warehouse after all."

"What?" Lt. Richards yelled back into the phone as he immediately stood up from his nice plush comfortable woodgrain desk.

"Yes sir, it seems as though they were killed somewhere else and then placed at the warehouse to make it seem as if they were actually killed there."

"And how did you come up with that scenario, young man?" Lt. Richards asked as his face began to turn beet red.

"Due to the body parts that seemed to be missing, one of the officers were shot in the front portion of his cranium.

And the problem with that sir is that we never found the top portion of his cranium."

"What?" Lt. Richards asked in disbelief.

"Head, sir and then the second officer we found was shot in the back of his cranium."

"Let me take a wild fucking guess, you never found the back of his cranium either?"

"Correct sir, nor did we find any of his brain fragments either."

"Oh my God, so what your telling me is that my two officers were executed?"

The young man hesitated once again before reciting. "Sir, not only were they both executed, they were literally slaughtered as if they were dirty pigs. They were shot at point blank range, meaning that whomever shot Officer Protho also had portions of his brains splattered all over them."

"Who else have you shared this information with Officer Charles?"

"No one."

"Okay, keep a lid on this and I'll get back to you. I have a meeting with one of the victim's family to settle some agreements so that they don't sue the department."

"I do understand sir, but I can only keep this quiet for so long, sir. These two officers' families are gonna want to see the autopsy report, so that we can show their cause of death."

"They can wait. As it looks right now, we have two crooked cops who were trying to extort money and cars, not to mention two brand new homes from someone out there in the community of Metro West. So as far as I'm concerned, the case is considered closed. The autopsy can be put on hold until after the burials." Lt. Richards then hung up the phone before the forensic lab tech could say goodbye.

"Yes sir, thank you sir and have a nice day," the tech uttered with a bit of sarcasm in his voice as he looked at the phone and then slammed it back down on the base of it.

Just as Lt. Richards had sat back down at his desk, placing his hand over his wrinkled forehead, Sharon, her mother and aunt were walking inside of the police station all dressed down in black along with some dark Versace shades on their face making it seem as if they had been crying parts of the day.

Chapter 33
The Wilkerson Family.

Sharon, being the one who always took charge of any situation put before her, stepped in front of her family members and uttered, "Excuse me ma'am."

"Yes, can I help you?" the small, frail white woman asked.

Sharon took a firm stare at the small frail woman who looked like she should've been at home tending to a house full of grandchildren instead of being bent over some desk at the police station. "Yes, someone by the name of Mrs. Dunbar called me earlier and asked us if we could be here by two this afternoon."

"Oh yes, you must be Ms. Conoly, correct?"

"Yes ma'am and this is my mother and aunt."

The small woman quickly gathered her things from the desk and walked around to greet them. "Okay, please take a seat. Mrs. Dunbar will be with you all shortly. Is there anything that I can get you all while you wait here for her?" the woman asked as Sharon and her family sat down in the cold, stale, plain looking waiting area, thinking on what was about to be said to them while they anticipated the arrival of Mrs. Dunbar.

"No ma'am, thank you. I hope they don't have us down here all day, because I have to pick up Breanna from the daycare," Sharon said to her mother after she had thanked the woman for assisting them. Her mother crossed her legs as she looked back over at Sharon before replying, "Why didn't you have Joyce pick her up?"

"Because mom, every time you ask Joyce to do something, she will have her hands sticking out for something in return."

All her mother could do was shake her head in agreement, all while sitting there looking like her and Sharon could be sisters.

Now the aunt, who was Do-Dirty's mother, stood around five foot seven, weighing around one hundred and eighty five pounds with a very dark skinned complexion and a very nasty attitude. I guess it came from her having so many kids to look after and never having enough time or money to take care of them. But with the money she was about to receive from Do-Dirty being murdered by the cops, she would be well taken care of, for the rest of her natural born life.

"Good afternoon, I'm Mrs. Dunbar. You all must be the Conoly family?"

"No, Sharon's last name is Conoly. I'm Ms. Wilkerson and this is my sister and her daughter." Sharon's aunt stated as they all stood to follow Mrs. Dunbar back down the hall to her office.

"Excuse me, I'm so sorry. I'm also sorry for us meeting on these terms. Would you all please follow me to my office," she said as she led the family down the hall towards her office.

They then followed behind Mrs. Dunbar, who was a beautiful black woman who weighed around a hundred and forty five pounds with a very light skinned complexion along with a college girls figure. She stood around five foot eight and couldn't be no older than thirty five years of age with a head full of long, black, silky hair. Her figure made her stand out in a crowd with the way it looked like she worked out every day. In other words, her body looked very toned as the way it hugged her in her police uniform.

"Come right on in and have a seat please."

"Thank you, ma'am, and thanks for your concern in regards to our family member being lost at the hands of some of your officers," Sharon replied as they took their seats inside of Mrs. Dunbar's plush window view office that was decorated with numerous awards and citations of merit, that she had received throughout her lustrous career with the department.

Chapter 34

A Million Dollars!

Mrs. Dunbar waited until everyone had been seated when she cleared her throat and then recited. "I want to thank you all for coming down to the station on such short notice. And once again I would like to send out our sincere condolences to your family for your loss. We all know how it feels when losing a family member."

Sharon's aunt cut in as she tried to hold back her emotions. "But not when you lose someone at the hands of the people you trust the most with your life!" Her sister then placed her arms around her sister as she whispered. "It's alright, the culprits behind her murder got what they deserved!"

"Once again, we want to apologize and we feel your pain," Mrs. Dunbar uttered as she looked away in the direction of Sharon, who was sitting there holding her composure.

"Thank you once again for your kind words and thoughts. I speak for the entire family when I tell you how grateful we are that you all have thought about us in our time of need," Sharon said to Mrs. Dunbar as she gave her aunt a tissue to wipe away the tears that were trekking down her face.

"With that being said, Ms. Conoly, let me cut right through the chase. The department would like to settle everything out of court, so it would help with the burial of your loved one. Have you all hired an attorney yet?"

"No ma'am, and the deceased family member was my youngest daughter," Sharon's aunt blurted out to Mrs. Dunbar as she continued wiping away tears from her crying eyes.

"Please excuse me, Ms. Wilkerson, once again I'm so sorry for your loss. We're willing to offer your family eight hundred and fifty thousand dollars along with paying for the burial of your daughter."

"And how much of that would we receive if the matter was handled in court?" Sharon's aunt quickly asked as Sharon and her mother sat there waiting on Mrs. Dunbar to reply.

"I really couldn't give you a specific amount, but please consider this. If you all went to court you would have to hire legal representation and they would get at least half of whatever the settlement amount would be. Also, the different families involved would be included in the lawsuit. Meaning that you all would have to split the one amount agreed upon. But if you take this check today, you all wouldn't have to split one red cent."

They all looked around at each other when Sharon turned to Mrs. Dunbar and asked her, "Okay, what about Bernard "Fats" Walker, it seems like those same two crooked ass cops of yours had their hands in his death as well?"

"That name hasn't come across my desk yet as a connected homicide, to this particular case ma'am," Mrs. Dunbar replied as a quizzical look crossed her face.

"Don't worry, it will," Sharon sarcastically replied, while rolling her eyes in the direction of Mrs. Dunbar.

"Well, if and when that happens we'll definitely take care of it. Hopefully he will be found unharmed in the near future. But if it's determined at a later date that they had something to do with his disappearance or murder, we would be more than happy to compensate your family."

"Well, if you all could make the check out for a million dollars, we would be fine with that," Sharon's aunt replied to Mrs. Dunbar as Sharon cut her eyes over at her aunt with a surprised look on her face.

"Ma'am, please understand I'm not at liberty to bargain with you I would have to speak to the department heads and then go from there."

"Okay and how long will that process take?"

"Give me a minute, Ms. Wilkerson and I'll be right back with your answer. Would you all like some coffee or tea while you wait?" Mrs. Dunbar asked as she got up from her desk.

"No ma'am, we're fine."

As Mrs. Dunbar left the room, Sharon abruptly turned to her aunt with. "Auntie let's just take the money and get out of here. When they realize that those two officers had something to do with Uncle Bernard too, we'll be right back down here collecting another fat ass check. With the money you're about to receive right now, you can pay back Michael and still have enough to take care of you and the family."

"You're absolutely right my dear, but it was my baby daughter and there is still not enough money for her children that are left behind, " Sharon's aunt replied while standing up looking out of the office window.

Five minutes later Mrs. Dunbar walked back into her office with a smile on her gorgeous looking face.

"Okay, looks like you all will be getting a nice check for a million dollars!"

Chapter 35

House Full Of Kids!

That Friday afternoon, the girls all decided to go ahead onto Jacksonville without me. Due to me attending Do-Dirty's funeral that Saturday morning., I would eventually meet up with them that Saturday afternoon and then go to our Bachelor Party from there. So, in the meantime, that Friday night was spent alone with no one other than Sharon. After the traditional fish fry, that was held over at her place with her immediate family members, Sharon and I ventured back over to my humble abode for the evening. We got in around eleven that mid summers night, with Sharon darting off to my bathroom so that she could tie her four hundred dollar hairdo up, that she didn't want to sleep on before the funeral.

"Michael, did you see Tamika at the house with her two beautiful kids?" She asked me from around the corner of the bathroom.

"I'm not sure, due to all the people that were in attendance. I really didn't notice her or her kids," I replied back to her trying not to give myself away.

"Well, she was there, and the reason why I asked was because of her cute lil daughter that she had with her. She looked so cute in her lil Baby Phat outfit."

"For real?" I replied back to her while trying to focus on ESPN and what Stuart Scott the announcer was saying about my Dallas Cowboys upcoming football season.

"Yes, I can't wait until we have a lil girl so that I can dress her up, so that we look like twins whenever we go out together."

I raised up in bed as I yelled back to her in confusion. "I thought that you said that we were having a boy?"

She quickly replied, "I know Michael, I'm talking about when we have our second child."

"Damn, the kids, huh?" I asked.

"Yes. Is that a problem?" she asked from inside the bathroom.

"No," I replied.

"Michael, just watch television," she said, as if I didn't see Tamika and her kids.

The problem I had now was what if that beautiful little girl she had with her was mine? I was sure going to find the answer out sooner than later, due to what was about to transpire the following day.

Chapter 36

Fallen Soldier!

9:45AM Saturday morning had arrived just as fast as Friday evening had passed away. The funeral was only a few hours away and my head was spinning as I dully sat on the edge of my bed, dreading the notion of burying a fallen soldier.

The hideous idea of me having to bare to witness to her untimely departure was that I was the one to cause the soldier to have fallen.

As I sat there on the edge of my bed pondering over her departure, Sharon rolled over and placed her hand in the small of my back. She caught me by surprise as she softly whispered.

"What time is it bae?"

I reached for my time piece on the nightstand and then turned to her to say, "It's about that time sweetheart."

She stretched her arms out as she yawned and then uttered, "Ahh bae, let me get at least ten more minutes please."

"That's fine bae, do you," I replied as I tried to stand up to walk into the bathroom.

"Thank you bae," she said to me as she placed her arms around me, preventing me from walking away from her grasp. She then whispered into my ear lobe.

"I love you so much, Michael Vallentino."

"Yeah, ditto Sharon."

"Whatever Michael," she muttered as she rolled back over in her favorite spot in my bed.

I then proceeded into the bathroom, so that I could shave before jumping into the shower. Promptly after shaving I went to check on Firstborn, to make sure that the limo was ready for the funeral. I knocked twice on his bedroom door and then walked inside of the room.

He was just walking out of the bathroom when I hit him with. "Good morning Firstborn, are you busy?"

He looked up at me and smiled as he replied, "Nah lil bro, just making sure I look the part when I put on this brand new tailored, fitted Armani suit, that's all." His fat face glowed as he turned to look at me and then back at his thousand dollar suit that I had tailored especially for him. Since we were brothers, we might as well had went to the funeral looking our very best.

"Is everything inside the limo?" I asked as I walked over to his window.

"Yes, I had the seats removed and replaced them with brand new seats, along with a new console and new carpet on the floor," he replied as I turned back towards him and asked.

"And how much did all that cost me?"

"Around five racks my brother. But you don't have to worry about paying for it."

"And why is that Firstborn?" he then looked at me as if I was dumb or slow.

"Baby Boy, do you think I'm stupid or something? Whatever money that them two idiots didn't throw at the ladies, I ended up keeping for us."

"That would be all good and shit if the police didn't keep all the serial numbers to the evidence money, smart guy!"

He then looked at me as though I had just pulled out my pistol and told him to put his hands up. "Mike, are you for real?" I cut a sinister grin back at him and then said, "Man, you good. Now, remember after the funeral we have to get on the road headed to Jacksonville and then over to Jasper for that Bachelor Party."

"No problem, are we staying the night or driving back after the Bachelor Party?"

"It all depends on how big that nigga's house is and how things turn out."

"Okay, well whatever you decide Baby Boy, I'm good with."

CHAPTER 37
MY APPEARANCE!

I had just turned to walk out of his room when I heard Sharon screaming from down the hallway. Her voice echoed throughout the somewhat quiet house as she screamed. "Michael, Michael!"

I turned back towards my brother and said. "Damn, you know who that is. Be ready with the limo in about an hour."

"Alright, Baby Boy," he replied as I reached the entrance of his bedroom door. I turned back towards him with my signature smile smeared across my face and uttered, "By the way Firstborn, your suit looks nice."

He looked up at me with his broad smile and then muttered, "Thanks Baby Boy. But we all know that your suit is gonna be off the chain."

"We'll see," I replied as I closed his door, then yelling back to Sharon. "Yes Sharon, I'm on the way, beautiful.

While walking back to my room, I was thinking to myself as how nice it was to finally see my brother in something besides a pair of pants and a T-shirt.

Firstborn stood around five foot eleven and weighing around two hundred and five pounds. His skin complexion was a light brown caramel color. Most people would say that he looked more like our father than I did. I would agree with them. As we both grew older, he did start to look more like dad than I did. Even with him not ever playing any organized sports in his entire life, he still had an athletic body frame. In which I guess he got from the many different years that he spent throughout the Florida State Prison system. Whatever the reason he always made sure that he stayed in some type of physical shape.

Our father would have been thrilled to see us together, working side by side as brothers should be. But due my strenuous work habits, time never permitted the both of us to visit the old man as much as we would have preferred too.

I opened my bedroom door as the sight of seeing Sharon standing there in her Guess lingerie, brought me back to reality. She was standing there looking like a runway model. Even though she was having my child, her flawless body still maintained its natural beauty and shape.

Only thing that was changing was her lil cute, poked out belly. Just by looking at her in the mirror, caused my manhood to rise. Only if we would have had more time. I would have started up once more with her, but time was of the essence as I said to her standing there looking back at me.

"What's wrong baby girl. Why aren't you dressed yet?"

"Because I needed your help big head. I need you to help me fasten up my bra. With me being with child now my damn titties are getting bigger and bigger every day. It seemed as though I could fit my bra around these melons on my chest with a lil help from you.

"Sorry baby, do you still need my help?" I asked as I stood there fantasying about making love to her.

"I got it now, thanks anyway," she replied as I darted off for the shower. I knew that it was getting closer to us departing the house, so I was in and out in no time.

Sharon was over in the mirror while I was over by the walk in closet putting the final touches to one of my Morris Day tailored made suits.

As I bent over tying up my all white Stacey Adams, Sharon looked at me and said, "Now don't you look stunning, young man!"

I stood there in my mirror gazing at myself before answering back with, "Thank you Sharon, you know that I have to make sure I keep my appearance tight at all times."

She walked over and stood next to me with the both of us staring at ourselves in the mirror.

Chapter 38
Family Portrait!

I was dressed in all white, while Sharon stood next to me with an all-white Bottega Veneta silk dress on, along with a nice pair of white high heel Prada shoes. She looked up at me with us both still in gazing at ourselves in the mirror and said, "Now don't we look nice together?"

"Yes, that we do, Sharon."

"So when are we going to take pictures together as a family, Michael?"

I bent down and kissed her on her cheeks as I uttered. "Just as soon as you have my son. We're going to take some nice family pictures then."

She smiled back at me and then said, "That will be nice, I can't wait."

Thirty minutes later, there was a knock at my bedroom door.

"Yo, Baby Boy, it's about that time my brother."

"We'll meet you downstairs. Have the limo on and ready to leave." I shouted back to him.

Five minutes later, he was opening the rear passenger door of the limo for Sharon and I to get in. I couldn't tell if she was crying or not due to her eyes being concealed by some Dolce Gabbana sunglasses. Neither could she tell what was going on with my eyes either, due to them being covered by a pair of black Gucci Shades.

Firstborn whipped that big nice white plush limo out onto the street. He made a right at the light onto Kirkman headed to I-4, when she looked to me and said.

"Oh, before I forget, remind me to give you a check for the cost of the funeral when we get back to my house."

"Excuse me?" I asked her with a surprised expression written over my face.

"My bad, I thought that I told you already."

"Told me what, Sharon?"

"They gave us a million dollars for taking the life of my cousin. And her mother gave me a blank check to fill out for the cost of the funeral that you paid for."

"Damn, a million dollar settlement huh?" I replied as I stared out of the window in disbelief.

"Yep a cool million dollars. How much did Coney Brothers charge you anyway?" She asked as she slid down her shades.

"It was a pretty penny. Even though Sonya and I went to school together, she still hit me in the pockets for the burial of lil ole Do-Dirty."

"Well your money will be refunded to you as soon as we get to my house," she replied as she laid her head on my shoulders. I then leaned my head back as well and relished the moment of Sharon and I both being alone together in the backseat of the limo. The limo I was about to make mine, due to all the turmoil that the limo had been put through.

Chapter 39
Mykel Essence Vallentino!

Once we arrived at Sharon's house, everyone was already there waiting for us, so that we could all follow behind one another to the church. Firstborn and I did the usual when we emerged from the limo, which was greeting the different family members upon are arrival.

With Sharon inside checking on her aunt and mother, I stood off to the side talking and meeting with the rest of the family. While standing there I could feel the eyes of Tamika staring at me from afar.

That's when I tapped Firstborn on the shoulder and said. "Hey, you see that fine ass female over there talking with the older guy?"

Firstborn was busy getting an eye full of the beautiful women in attendance when he
turned and replied. "Yeah, I saw her pointing over this way several times already. What's up, do you know her?"

"Yeah, it seems as though I used to mess around with her back in the day."

"Okay, so who invited her to the funeral? I know you didn't," he replied while looking confused, as he sipped from his cold can of Pepsi soda, held firmly in the palm of his hand.

"Nah, silly ass man. It seems as though her and Sharon are somehow related to one another."

"Damn, that's fucked up!" he muttered.

"I know, tell me about it. That's not all though. The female claims that we have a daughter together."

He looked back at me and then uttered, "Damn Baby Boy, you about as bad as me when it comes to the kids, aren't you?"

"Whatever homie," I replied as the young boy who I had met at Sharon's place only a few days ago came running over to Firstborn and I with the cutest lil girl I had ever seen.

"Excuse me Mister Michael."

We both looked down at the pair of kids standing before us. "Yes, what can I do for you and the lil princess here?"

They both looked up at me with wide shimmering eyes. At first I was caught off guard, but then I looked deep in the eyes of the young girl, who locked me in a trance as soon as I laid eyes on her. I was standing there stuck when I heard the young boy say.

"My sister wanted to meet her father." Pure adrenaline rushed to my head as Firstborn began to choke. I just stood there and said. "Excuse me?" I then kneeled down so I could hear the young girl speak, as she softly whispered.

"Hello daddy."

I was shocked or should I say amazed as this lil cute precious, young female who couldn't be no older than six, called me her father.

"Hello, beautiful and what is your name?" I asked her as Firstborn still stood next to me choking.

"Mykel Essence Vallentino," she replied as her beautiful name rolled off of her lips.

I slowly stood up, reciting to myself. "Damn, her mother gave her the same initials as I. Michael Eric Vallentino!' A single tear of joy began to snake down the right side of my cheek as I picked her young petite body up off of the ground and placed her inside of my arms.

There was no doubt in my mind as to her being my daughter, because she resembled my first daughter Shakina and even looked a bit like my second daughter Aerial.

"My mommy said that you would be here today. Why haven't you ever came to see me before?" she asked me as she pulled on my ear lobe.

I turned to look her in her innocent face and said, "Mykel my dear, it's a long story baby girl. One that I will have to explain to you one day when we have some free time to talk to one another."

She looked at me with those bright eyes of hers and asked. "Okay, what about right now or is it a bad time daddy?"

Chapter 40
Smooth Ass!

I was still somewhat induced and a bit nervous about what was going on around me as I looked her directly in her eyes and said, "It's really not the place nor time sweetheart, but rest assure, I will make time for you at the first available moment that I have."

The entire time that I had her in my arms, her brother stood there staring at the both of us talking, when he blurted out with. "I wish that you were my daddy to Mister Michael."

I smiled as I looked at the young lad, when his mother Tamika came from around the corner, acting surprised and just as shocked as I was that her kids had cornered me off.

"What are you two doing over here bothering Mr. Michael?" She asked both of her kids, who were standing there stuck in awe.

I very calmly looked at Tamika and uttered. "Whatever, Tamika, you know that you sent these beautiful kids over here to me."

Tamika stood there acting as innocent as she could while smiling and blinking her right eye at the same time. She then stood firm and recited. "I thought that it was time that you finally met your daughter." She then took Mykel out of my arms while I snapped back with.

"But not here around family. Tamika, why couldn't you have just brought her over to my house?"

"Not around all those naked ass girls that you have running around your place!" She replied sarcastically.

"Naked girls!" her son shouted out loud as a wicked grin emerged on his face.

"Be quiet lil Michael, with your mannish lil ass!" Tamika shouted back as the young man continued smiling while thinking about my house full of naked girls.

"Tamika, let me call you after the funeral, so that Mykel and I can spend some time together."

"Can I come too, Mister Michael?" her son asked now displaying a huge smile on his face.

"That's entirely up to your mother, young man."

Tamika looked down at him and then back up at me. "Okay Michael, I'll call you after the funeral. Until then, you kids come on here before my cousin Sharon comes running out here and have a fit, seeing you all with her man!"

Just as soon as she had uttered those words, Sharon came out of the house with her aunt and mother along with my check in her hand.

"Hey Tamika and there she is Michael! See how cute her lil daughter is?" My head dropped as the smile on my face turned into something totally different than before.

Firstborn seen the expression on my face as he whispered back into my ear. "Damn boy, let's see your smooth ass get out of this one!"

Chapter 41

Saved By The Bell!

I looked over at my gorgeous looking female and voiced. "I see Sharon. She is a beautiful lil girl isn't she?"

"Yes, that she is Michael. She almost looks as if she could be one of your daughters, with her looking like your oldest daughter, Shakina." I looked over at Tamika who was just as caught off guard as I was. She seen the joy and excitement in her cousin's eyes, when she jumped in with. "Hey Sharon, let me get these kids together so that we can all get to the funeral."

Sharon stood back up from bending down, playing with Mykel and recited. "Hey Tamika, girl they're fine. I just can't get over how much she looks like my Michael. Do you see the resemblance Michael?"

Damn, here it was that I was mystified once again as she asked me that question in front of Tamika and Mykel, who I guess thought that I was about to disclaim her.

I cleared my throat and then said. "Yes Sharon. I might as well tell you now, before you hear it later in these damn streets. Sharon she looks like me because she is my."

"Come on everybody, can I have you all gather around so that we can pray together before leaving for the funeral?" Sharon's aunt said to the family members that were standing outside by now ready to head to the church.

I was saved by the bell as Firstborn looked at me and wiped his brow of the sweat that had started protruding over his face. "Boy you dodged a bullet just then!"

I looked back at him and said. "Shut up nigga!"

Sharon grabbed me by the hand as she led me away looking at me and wondering what I was about to say to her.

Meanwhile, Lil Mykel was waving bye to me as her mother led them away. Mykel made sure that we maintained eye contact as she motioned with her cute lil mouth. "I love you daddy."

I was touched. It wasn't until I heard Sharon's voice in my ear as she reached out to me with my check in her hand. "Here Michael, this is your check that I was telling you about." I was so taken away by my beautiful daughter that I barely heard her as I looked down to take the paper check from her hand.

"Thank you beautiful, but this could have waited until another time," I sputtered to her as I placed the check into my coat pocket and then stared at her Nia Long looking ass. "So, Michael, what was it that you were about to tell me back there?" she asked as we stood about to bow our heads for prayer.

"Nothing, I'll tell you later." I quickly brushed her off and then bowed my head for the family to pray together. The prayer was touching as it was also heart felt. I actually shed a few tears as I stood there thinking about Do-Dirty and questioning the actions that I had to take against her.

Just as the Rev Gallon had finished praying, I lifted up my head to spot Richard off to the side standing with his two daughters, looking nervous and out of place.
He saw us walking over to the limo and walked up to me dressed in an all-black suit with a white shirt and black tie, with a pair of Karl Kani shoes to match his ensemble.

"Hey cuz, can my daughters and I ride along with you all to the funeral?" We had just got to the rear door of the limo, when I turned back towards him looking like a younger version of Denzel Washington. I slid down my shades and said. "Of course, cousin, I wouldn't have it any other way."

"Man thanks, because I didn't want to have to drive my truck with all those girls shoes and stuff inside of it to the funeral."

"Don't mention it man. Go ahead and get in. We don't want to be late!"

Soon as Firstborn went to close the door, he looked at me and asked me. "Are you good?"

"As long as my big brother is with me I can't be nothing but okay."

He closed the door as I lowered my head down and got in sitting next to Sharon.

The doors to the limo had closed as I made myself comfortable as I sat next to Sharon, while Richard and his two lovely daughters sat off to the side of the limo patiently waiting for our arrival to the church, where they would see their dear departed mother for the very last time.

Sharon was sitting all up under me while I was busy looking out of the window, trying not to look at the kids of the person that I had sent to an early grave. Sharon's head laid there on my shoulder as I could hear her sniffling to herself.

I turned my head towards her and said. "Are you okay?"

"Yes Michael, I just really miss her!"

"I know you do, hell we all do."

She looked up at me with those dark shades on and then said. "Why did she have to have such a fucked up life?"

I positioned myself next to her and then whispered back into her ear. "Sharon, we all make some bad choices in our lifetime, you can't beat yourself up for the mistakes another person decides on making."

She then laid her head back down as she said. "I guess you're right, Michael. I just wish that I could have talked to her before she had to lose her life over something so stupid."

"Sometimes life deals us a shitty hand, either you play it to win or you play to lose. Either way someone has to lose. Just make sure that it isn't you who finds them self the one who lost!"

She held my hand tightly as she whispered. "Michael, I love you so much, please don't ever leave me." Her tears had begun to snake down her face as I gently tried to wipe them away.

"As long as I have breath in my lungs, I'm not going anywhere, beautiful."

"Alright you two, we're supposed to be going to a funeral, not a wedding," Richard cut in with as he looked at Sharon and I, who by now were holding on to one another as if it was one of us leaving.

"You're right cousin, sorry," I replied as I looked over at him.

"No problem cuz, once again thanks for allowing us to ride with you. Me and the girls just didn't want to ride along in that crowded limo with the rest of the immediate family."

"I understand partner, don't mention it. I'm just glad that I was able to be there for you and the girls," I replied as his younger daughter held onto something shining in her hand that seemed intriguing to her.

"Look daddy, didn't mom have one of these just like it?" She asked as Richard and I looked at what the young girl held in her hand.

"Let me see that." I had leaned up in my seat causing Sharon to move as well, when he asked his daughter for what it was that she held in her outstretched hand.

"My God, it's Do-Dirty's necklace that I bought for her on her last birthday!" he recited as he held it in his hand.

"What?" Sharon asked in confusion.

"It's the necklace that I bought for Do-Dirty on her last birthday," he said as I just sat there stunned and mystified on how it got there.

Seconds later is when all hell broke loose. Sharon and Richard both looked at me with one question on their uncertain state of mind.

"Michael, how did her necklace end up in your limo?"

Chapter 42

Thank You, Murder Queens!

Meanwhile... the girls had danced that Friday night back at Black Magic, but on the way to Jacksonville that Friday afternoon, Chyna was still somewhat bitter about the way those guys had treated her and White Chocolate, the weekend prior.

"Hey, I might know someone who knows how to get in touch with those females who call themselves the Murder Queens," Strawberry said to Chyna as they all sat there talking amongst one another.

"Girl, didn't you all hear on the news the other day about those so called Murder Queens?" A nosey ass Lil Kitty asked the girls while sitting there ear hustling on what Strawberry had just told Chyna.

"No, what happened now Miss Know it All?" a frustrated Charlie B asked Lil Kitty with an attitude towards her for getting them all kicked out of the Caribbean Beach Nightclub.

"They said that those two officers that got killed the other day were a part of the Murder Queens as well. Some people are even saying that those cops were parading around town wearing women clothing, while committing murders so that they could throw people off of their trail."

"Lil Kitty, please, who in the hell told you something like that?" Lil Red asked Lil Kitty while laughing at her wild and crazy story.

"For real girl, you didn't see it on the news?" Tameia said.

In the meantime, while clearing her throat, Suga Bear chimed in with. "She's right, it was on the news. I saw the report as well."

"Well, all I'm saying that if you girls know how to get in touch with anyone who knows who the real people are and how to get in touch with whomever, I will pay for their services," Chyna said to the truck load of women with anger in her voice and face.

The entire time that Chyna was talking with Strawberry and the other girls, Mignon, Nicole and of course, Entyce sat there quietly listening to the conversation.

That Friday night, they tell me that things were going fine until after the club, when those same two guys who had their way with Chyna and White Chocolate ran into the Murder Queens.

It seemed as though after the club closed that night, some of the girls went back to the hotel.

But four of the girls whose names I will not say, claimed that they had dates with two guys.

Those same two unlucky fellows took those four girls to some old nasty run down hotel off of Interstate 10 headed towards Lake City. That was the last time that anyone saw those two guys alive ever again.

That Saturday morning the news reported how a hotel maid went to open the room so that she could clean it, when she found the bodies of two men slain to death.

The murder was so gruesome that some of the details I'm about to tell you may not want to be read. Both victims had their individual manhood cut off and placed on the other one. The first victim had his homie's manhood stuck off inside of his mouth, while his partner had his homies manhood stuck up his shitty ass.

The police described the crime scene as a horrific crime of passion, that should have never went down in the way that it did.

"No one should have ever had to die like the way those two individuals died that early Saturday morning," the homicide detective said to one of the news reporters there at the hellish crime scene.

The police said that what baffled them the most was that no money was removed off of the victims. Just a note that

read. *'Don't go around fucking with the wrong women or you might just end up like these two punk ass niggas!'*

To this very day, the unsolved murder of Herman Julius Thigpen and Gerald June Bug Johnston has never been solved.

Now by the time you all have read this book, we all just might know what may have happened to them brothers that dreaded Saturday morning when they thought that tricking females out of their money and that prized possession between their legs; caused them their simple ass life.

All Chyna said after she found out was, "Thank you Murder Queens!"

Chapter 43

Whatever Happens In The Dark!

I was sitting there in that Limo flustered. First, I was furious at Firstborn for not finding the damn necklace in the first place. Then, I was mad at myself, because it was me who had seen her last before her last time breathing on Yahweh's green earth.

It was no time for me to be angry at the moment. I had to think fast, or the gig was up. Richard would know the truth and Sharon would know that it was I who had seen her cousin last.

"Let me see that please," I said to Richard who acted as if he couldn't let it go.

"Michael, Michael, do you want to explain how my cousin's necklace is here in this damn limo?" Sharon asked as she inched away from me.

Meanwhile, I was just sitting there with the necklace in my hand, staring at it, when I shouted out to Firstborn.

"Yo, Firstborn, didn't you say that you had the limo cleaned out?"

He slid down the partition and then said as he held a sinister grin on his face. "I did, but last night I had one of my lady friends in the back seat with me. That's her necklace. She informed me earlier this morning that she thought that she had lost it or somehow misplaced it. Who found it?"

"I did." the youngest girl yelled in excitement.

"Why thank you my child? I thought that I was going to have to buy ole girl another one. Here take this for finding it for me." Firstborn cool and collectively reached in his pocket and pulled out a crisp hundred dollar bill and handed it to the young girl.

"Ugh, thank you sir!" she yelled in excitement.

"I want one too!" her older sister yelled.

"Here, why not," Firstborn said as he handed her one too.

"Thank you." she said as a smile appeared on her face.

"No problem, thank you and your lil sister."

The young girl took the money as the partition went back up.

"Wow, what a small world huh, Richard?" he looked at me and then uttered. "It sure is cuz. Hey, I'm sorry if I seemed off key with you.

"No problem cousin, I don't know why you guys would think any different. You know that your girl used to work with the girls and I. That could have been hers and she could have actually left it in here one night after a show." I said as I adjusted my tie and then slid back in my seat, all while looking at Sharon.

"Your right , my bad."

"We all good cuz. Man sit back and relax. We should be at the church in a few."

"Thanks cuz."

"Now why were you looking at me as if I had did something wrong?" I asked Sharon as I pulled her in closer to
me.

"It's nothing Michael, I just wanted to know the answer as well."

"Whatever Sharon, I don't know what would make you think that I had something to do with your cousins death in the first place," I said to her as I kissed her on her lips.

"I don't know, Michael. Something just seems out of place. All I know is whatever happens in the dark, will one day come to the light!"

Chapter 44

Pine Box!

The church parking lot was packed with guests and friends as Firstborn slowly pulled into the large parking lot.

Richard's head was on a swivel as he stared out of the window, noticing all the cars and people lined up to enter inside the huge religious building.

"Wow, I didn't know that Do-Dirty had all these friends," he said as he turned back to look at me.

"For real, it seems like everybody came out to pay their respects to poor old Tonya," I replied.

"I see," he said as he held his youngest daughter close to him. The poor child looked as if she had been crying all morning.

"Humph, and I bet the person or persons responsible for her death are probably here too!" Sharon voiced as she peered out of the window, with an evil growl on her face.

"They probably are baby, they probably are," I said as I continued to sit there as if I didn't know who that person was.

"So Mike, why isn't any of your girls here to pay their respects to her?" she said as she turned her head toward me, still holding the angry growl on her face.

"They had a show in Jacksonville and then from there they have to be in Jasper. Matter of fact, after the funeral is over I have to be headed to Jacksonville so that I can be with them. You know how I hate for them to be on the road without me."

"Whatever, them hoes could have at least shown their faces here at her funeral. If you ask me, they know what happened to my cousin," Sharon said as she began to make sure she looked okay before she stepped out of the limo.

"C'mon Sharon, don't start. We have already been there with that notion. What makes you think that they had something to do with her murder anyway?"

"It's just the gut feeling that I have. Now move so we can get out of this damn limo."

Firstborn had just parked the limo in front of the religious building as we began looking over ourselves.

"Okay guys, we're here," he said as he opened the rear door.

Richard and his daughters got out first, with Sharon and me getting out right behind them.

Thank you," Richard uttered as he stepped out.

"No problem, sorry about your loss."

They briefly hugged one another as his two daughters stood there next to their father, looking like they were about to start crying.

"Thanks for getting us here safe my good man," I said to Firstborn as Sharon and I were stepping out of the limo.

"Don't mention it. Is this spot okay for the limo?"

"Yes. Just as long as we can get out of here as soon as the funeral is over," I replied.

"Cool."

Richard and his daughters walked ahead of us as Firstborn and I stood there talking.

"C'mon Michael, we have to get in line with the family!" Sharon yelled as she stood there waiting on me.

"Sorry bae, here I come." I shouted back to her. I then turned back to Firstborn and said. "Thanks for thinking fast on your feet earlier. Man we have to be more careful. For some reason, Sharon seems very suspicious."

Just as I had finished talking, I hear. "Your damn right I seem suspicious, and Firstborn don't think for one minute that I believe that bullshit ass story you came up with earlier. For one, your ass was home all night. I know that because I stayed the night, remember? Now Michael, bring your ass on!"

Firstborn and I looked at one another while shaking our head in doubt of what we had just heard coming out of her mouth. I had turned away trying to catch up to her when I reached out and grabbed for her hand. She still being angry, immediately snatched her hand away as I played off the embarrassing moment.

Firstborn was still standing by the door of the limo. He had just closed the door when he muttered to himself. Alright bitch, don't end up like your cousin, because before you take me or my brother out, I'll have that fine ass yours, resting nicely in a freshly made pine box!"

Chapter 45

I Feel Like Going Home!

I was walking next to Sharon with smoke steaming from her head. I could sense that she was still mad and upset, especially since she overheard the conversation between my brother and I.

With the way things were going and the vibe that she had sent out, I knew that it would only be a matter of time before things would go south for her and I. In the meantime, I would have to try my best to keep her from finding out the truth about her cousin's murder.

The closer we got to the entrance of the church is when I reached out and pulled her closer to me. Just as I had placed my arms around her nice, elegant body, she fell into my arms. I guess the sight of all the people already inside startled her. I looked down at her and said. "What's wrong, is everything okay?"

She looked around at first like she was out of breath. Then, she looked back up at me and faintly said, "Yes bae, please forgive me. For a minute there, I thought that I was going to faint or pass out."

"See, and just a minute ago you snatched your hand away from me like you didn't need me here with you."

"Boy shut up and walk with your lady. And you're damn right. Hell, I can't help it if I think that you and your slick ass brother has something to hide."

"Whatever Sharon, like I said, we have or should I say, had nothing to do with anything! Now be quiet so we can take our seats"

"Whatever," she uttered as they sat us right next to her mother. Her mother was already seated, looking lovely as ever, dressed in a nice all black Gloria Vertard dress. She slightly turned towards Sharon and I and then gave us a quick nod of approval at our arrival.

I leaned across Sharon and said to her mother. "My sincere condolences to your family." She looked back at me and I could have sworn that I was looking at a slightly older version of Sexy Redd.

"Thank you Michael, and once again thank you for all the help and support you have offered the family. All of this would not have been made possible if it wasn't for you."

I nodded my head as I leaned back up against the nice leathered pew that we were all seated in. "Damn, did she have to put it like that!" I said to myself under my breath.

Sharon pulled down her shades and then looked up at me and said, "I know that's right, just think Mister. If it wasn't for you, none of this would be taking place."

I tried to smile but then I knew what she was trying to insinuate. "Yeah Sharon, your mother has already thanked me enough," I replied sarcastically.

She then slid next to her mother placing her arm around her and consoling her as the choir began to sing I Feel Like Going Home by Bishop Marvin Winans. It was supposed to be Do-Dirty's favorite song.

The choir had the crowd crying and shouting already. The service hadn't even begun yet as a few of Do-Dirty's family members began shouting and screaming. Hell, one lady fell out of her seat rolling her fat ass into the isle of the church. She was rolling on the floor shaking her legs and just acting a damn fool as the choir took off.

And then, like someone had told his fake ass to get up, The Honorable Rev. Travis Elrod Gallon jumped and began shouting. "I feel like going home, church do you hear me!"

Man, people all over the church began shouting for joy and crying, like they were having Sunday service, yelling and screaming, shouting and jumping for joy. I mean it was a real homegoing service for ole girl.

Sharon even stood up and started clapping and sashaying her lil fine ass from side to side, while singing along with the choir. Before I knew anything, tears were racing down my face uncontrollably.

Chapter 46

Small Hand!

I couldn't believe what was happening to me at that very moment. All the cool in me had suddenly hauled ass, as I sat there balling like a grown baby. Sharon who was still standing there clapping and singing looked down and saw that I was crying and began crying even harder all while still sashaying that fine red ass of hers in front of me.

"Mike, Mike, are you alright?" my brother asked me as
he leaned up against the back of the pew, while handing me a handkerchief to wipe away my tears.

"Yeah, I'm good, thanks," I replied as I leaned over and started wiping away.

I had been bent over for a few seconds, wiping away the tears that wouldn't stop flowing, when I felt a small hand in the small of my back.

I dimly turned my head to the left, while witnessing the most beautiful sight a grown man would want to see. It was my daughter, precious little Mykel Essence Vallentino. We both locked eyes as she said, "I saw my daddy over here crying, so I told my mother that I was going to make sure he was okay. She tried to stop me but that fat lady who's rolling over in the isle got in her way."

I burst out laughing at what she had just said, when she looked at me puzzled and said, "What's so funny, dad?"

I didn't know if I wanted to cry or just keep laughing as I looked at her and said. "Girl, you're just as funny as your sister, Aerial!"

"What, I have a sister named Aerial?" she asked, sounding so excited and looking around, as if Aerial was actually there for her to see.

"Yes little one, and another sister named Shakina." I had just wiped away the last tear when she said.

"So when am I going to meet them?"

"Soon little one, very soon."

She smiled as I placed my arms around her and pulled her up under me.

"Alright boy, you know Ms. Thang is already thirty eight hot with your ass."

"I know Firstborn, I got this," I replied as Mykel looked back at my brother. She then looked back at me with a quizzical expression on her face.

"Who is that man daddy? He looks like you a lil bit?"

"That's your uncle. His name is James, but I call him Firstborn, since he was born first." She immediately turned around and waved at Firstborn
before she uttered. "Hey uncle Firstborn."

James just smiled back at her as the choir finished up singing the remix version of I Feel Like Going Home.

Sharon, who had been standing up the entire time that they had been singing, slowly sat back down and dully reached over and made sure her mother was alright. After helping her with her hat and young daughter Breanna, she looked over at me and said. "I see that you're okay. Now who is the little pretty lady sitting next to you?" Then looking at Mykel, smiling she said. "Are you trying to take my man from me?" with her face still holding a radiant bright smile.

Oh shit! Now I was really about to get it. I couldn't he rude to Mykel and tell her to beat it, so that Sharon wouldn't find out about my secret. Here I was now, once again, stuck. Only this time between Sharon and my newfound baby girl. So I took a brief sigh, cleared my throat and looked Sharon directly in those pretty eyes of hers and said. "Sharon, I was trying to tell you back at the house before we left, but your aunt interrupted me." I was carefully pulling Mykel closer to me. I went on to say. "This is Mykel."

Sharon's lovely smile grew larger as she simply said. "Hey Mykel, I already know you, because your my lil cousin." then softly wiping away at her tears that had stained her face.

Chapter 47
Rev. Travis Elroy Gallon

"Whew!" I said as I leaned back up against the pew bench.

"You didn't think that I knew that she was my cousin?" she asked.

Shaking my head, I was like. "Damn Sharon, how long have you knew about me knowing little Mykel?"

"Boy, we both have known, but here is not the place or time to be discussing this small matter. Later after the funeral, is when we will have this conversation. Now please place those arms of yours around me and make sure that I don't fall out like that fat lady in the back just did. The damn heifer isn't even a part of the family."

"What?" I asked trying to seem surprised, then swiftly turning my head in the woman's direction.

"Yes Michael, she just goes around to all of the other people's funeral and act out like that. They say that the poor lady is half crazy."

I then slowly turned back around to see the woman who was actually sitting in the back talking to herself. I then bent my head down towards Sharon and said. "Hey, she looks like she is actually talking to someone."

Sharon then densely turned to observe the woman. "They say that she be actually talking to the dead person who's funeral. she's at." Sharon said.

'Damn! I hope she ain't talking to Do-Dirty's ass.' I thought to myself. Then, looking back into Sharon's eyes. I said. "That's some crazy shit."

Firstborn then turned as well, to witness what Sharon and I were witnessing. After turning back around he was like. "Pss, yo bro, what's good? Ole girl ain't tripping out on you yet?"

Cool as I was, I looked back at him and recited. "Nah, seems as though she already knew, Mykel. She just doesn't know about her being my daughter."

He smirked then replied. "That's cold."
"Nah, what's cold is the old fat lady in the back who just fell out in the middle of the isle, screaming and carrying on."

Turning around again, to look for himself, then tapping me on the shoulder to say. "Who, that lady back there talking to herself?"

"Yeah, that one," I voiced still trying to maintain my composure. "Isn't she a part of their family?" he asked as he waited for my answer.

"No, she just shows up at people's funerals and then acts a fool up inside the church. They say that she does that so that she doesn't feel guilty while eating with the family after the funeral."

Sharon then interrupted the both of us with. "Now could you two be quiet, it's very rude to be talking at someone's funeral." Then turned her head back around to the front.

"You heard her playa."

"Yeah, whatever," Firstborn replied as he slid back into the seat, rolling his eyes at the back of Sharon's head.

Minutes later, the Pastor of the church stood up and recited. "Could I have everyone's attention please? If you have your bible with you, could you please turn with me and read the 23rd Psalm." The large number of people in attendance did as the Pastor asked and read the passage, after which he went on to say. "May God bless the readers and doers of his word. Now it does my heart good to introduce to some and to the ones who already know one of God's true Ministers, ladies and gentlemen please help me welcome the esteemed Minister Reverend Travis Elrod J. Gallon!"

Chapter 48
Off The Bone!

The funeral lasted damn there three hours with long winded ass Rev. Gallon talking until Tonya Latoya Wilkerson aka Do-Dirty stood up in her casket and said. "Damn man, you ain't done yet?"

During the funeral, Sharon tried to stand up and say something nice about her dearly departed cousin, but she had to sit back down while being overcome with grief.

I sat there holding my composure and stature after crying earlier as I listened to the different family members and friends talk about how their wonderful cousins life had been.

The funeral would have been okay if the damn Rev. Gallon hadn't been up their talking and preaching.

After we went to the burial site, we headed back to the church. Then after mingling with family and friends at the church, a few of the family members arrived back at Sharon's place for the family get together.

After a brief stint there, Firstborn and myself got on the highway headed towards Jacksonville. Sharon, of course wanted to come along for the ride, but I had met this one lil cute female at the church who had heard about the Hot Girls and wanted a job. So, I had her grab a few things at her house. Once she had her items, we hit the road. I gave her a quick interview inside the limo while Firstborn drove to Jacksonville.

The short cute, petite female was scrump delicious with
her beauty, style and grace. Her skin complexion was light red, just the way I liked them, short with a spunky lil attitude. Her height was around five foot four and she looked as though she weighed somewhere around a hundred and twenty-five pounds.

She held a nice firm breast size, looking like it was at least a thirty-four C cup. Yes, you could say that she was going to make a lot of money, so I decided on giving her the stage name Mo-Money.

As she started to undress in the back seat of the limo, my manhood was trying to check her out just as bad as my eyes were trying to see her beautiful body. Once she was fully naked, she looked at me and asked. "So how do I look, Mister Michael? Do you think that I will be able to make me some money?"

"Yes my dear, you're about to make some right now. Let's see how you eat the dick off of the bone, real quick."

Chapter 49
Small Ass Stomach!

The elegant young woman, who I had just picked up and convinced to come along for the ride, looked at me with a disarming wicked smile and said. "Excuse me?"

"Ahh, you know what I'm trying to say. Let's see how nice you are when it comes to placing the mouth on this quite large joystick!" I was shocked just as much as she was, due to me never being that direct with a female I had just met. Boy was I ever changing for the worst, I always showed the women mad respect. She sat there staring at me and my manhood for a few seconds before she said. "I'm so sorry, Mister Michael. I just don't kick my game like that, especially with me just meeting you and all. For one, I don't care how fine and handsome he looks, I'm just not sucking his dick!"

"My bad shorty, please excuse my arrogance," I replied feeling all rejected and shit.

Mo Money sat there rolling her cute small eyes at me and my erected manhood before she said. "But in your case, you're actually different from any other man that I've met before you, so I'm gonna suck all of that big fat long ass dick of yours as if my lil life depended on it!"

I gave her a weak smile as I positioned myself for what seemed like it was really about to go down in the back of that limo.

"Now, that's my girl. Bring your lil short ass over here!" That pretty lil red thang started sucking and blowing on my manhood as if we were a couple already. She had me asking her. "Damn girl, what in the hell are you trying to do to me?"

She looked up at me with half of my manhood emerged in her mouth and said. "Trying to show your handsome black ass how much I want this job and you!" She then went down as far as she could before choking on my shaft.

The feeling was like non other. Her young tender mouth felt so warm and delightful, while I just sat there enjoying the attention my manhood was receiving.

Her large ass head was bobbing back and forth, when I
placed my hands on her cheeks, pulling her head up. I looked her directly in the eyes and said. "Hell, you got the job as soon as you jumped your lil fine ass inside of the limo."

She just smiled and continued to please me and my manhood.

After thirty minutes of her doing me, it was time for me to suck the juices out of her wet, soaking ass pussy.
First, I laid her lil ass down on the seat and placed one of her legs up over the seat, while I gently placed her other leg up over my shoulder.

Then, I sucked on her Lil Man In The Boat clit as if it was a piece of hickory smoked bacon. Seconds later, it began to swell up inside of my mouth. After I had her eyes rolling in the back of her head is when I inserted my tongue deep inside of her wet vagina. At first, she tried to push my head back, but as soon as she sensed the pleasure I was giving her and her vagina, she just laid back and relaxed.

I then showed her why there was so many girls on the team, while my tongue went deeper and deeper into forbidden waters. I was so in tuned into what I was doing, that I actually started blowing in her sweet smelling ass on a few occasions.
I had one of my Pretty Ricky Porn flicks playing inside the television, so that she could see that I was a more fined professional than he was. I mean I was licking on the poor girl as if she was a hundred-dollar steak dinner.

After a few more deep breaths and two or three orgasms, I knew that it was time for me to place all ten and a half inches of my swollen manhood deep inside of her small ass stomach, where no other man had been.

The Murder Queens 4

Chapter 50
Damn!

As I gently took both of her legs and placed her knee caps up behind her ears, her small eyes began to enlarge at the sight of what was about to take place in her young life. I then slowly pushed as deep as I could inside of her soft stomach. It wasn't until she looked me directly in the eyes and said. "Now, you know damn well that you have too much dick up inside of my lil short ass! Hell your dick is just as tall as I am!"

I smiled and then grinned at her, before I said, "Well, by the time we get to Jacksonville, you should be at least grown a few inches taller." I continued smiling as I began punishing her lil fine ass. I made soft, bittersweet passionate love to her the only way I knew how all the way to Jacksonville. You Betta Believe It.

By the time we got off into Duval County, she was good and tired. Firstborn was pulling the limo up into the hotel parking lot around six that evening.

As Mo Money climbed out of the limo stumbling towards the hotel room, I placed my arms around her, catching her right before she fell to the pavement. Once I had my future princess firmly in my grasp, I looked at her and said. "Hey you, are you okay baby girl?"

She turned her head sideways and said. "Oh, now your ass wants to be all concerned and shit! Nah, I ain't alright. I can't feel my damn legs, Mister Michael!" She then latched on to my outstretched arm for balance and support.

"That's okay, you should get some feeling in them by the time you have to dance tonight," I said as we both walked side by side together, searching out the right room number for the ladies and I.

To save money for the weekend, all of the ladies decided to chip in on a suite, so that they all could be together in one room.

As Firstborn, Mo Money and I waltzed into their room, all of them were kicking back waiting on my arrival.

"Hey ladies, nice to see you all here. How is everybody doing?" I said to the large room of females gathered together for the weekend.

"We all good, Mike. We missed you. How was the funeral?" Chyna said to me as everyone was greeting Firstborn and Mo Money.

"Everything was fine Chyna. I missed you guys as well, even you Strawberry "

"Whatever Mike, how did my boo Richard take the funeral?" Strawberry asked me as Firstborn heard what she had said.

His head turned around as if he was the young girl from the Exorcist as he recited.

"Oh, so you gonna ask my brother about another nigga, right in front of my black ass?" His face held a serious ass unit as he spoke.

Strawberry quickly tried to cover up her mistake as she said. "Now you know how I feel about you. I was just asking boo. I meant no harm!"

"When I get off inside that lil tight asshole of yours tonight, you won't never think about another man for the rest of your natural born life!" She then looked around the room as if she was looking for some help, from one of the girls.

"Excuse me you two, can I please start the meeting now!"

"Mike, your brother is a real trip." Lil Red said all out loud as she continued laughing at what he had just said to Strawberry.

Chyna then raised her hand as if we were in school or something.

"Yes, Chyna, what is it?"

"Excuse me everyone, I would just like to say, who-ever contacted them Murder Queens for me, thanks. They really handled their business last night."

At first, the smile on my face quickly disappeared and then my eyes searched out the room for the four girls who I knew were a part of the infamous group.

"What?" I yelled.

"Yeah Mike, them hoes put in major work on them fools!" White Chocolate uttered out loud.

Them fools showed up here last night. The same ones that tried me and ole girl last time."

I just sat down and growled.

Chapter 51

Out Of Here!

I fell down hard into the chair seated behind me. Once I was sitting down, is when I placed my hand up against my temple, and began to ponder of the Murder Queens untimely actions.

The room was silent as I heard Mo Money utter out loud. "Damn, them bad ass bitches are up here too! I knew that I had heard about them down in Orlando, but not here in Jacksonville. So, you mean to tell me that Jacksonville has some of them hoes up here too?"

"No child, sit down!" I replied.

"Nah, his black ass knows who they are?" I looked in the direction where the remark had originated from and said.

"Shut the hell up, Suga Bear. Like I said before, I don't know who those females are. Now what in the hell happened up here last night?"

"It's been all over the news today, Mike. It seems as though whoever they are, got a hold of the same two lame ass brothers who took ole girl and Chyna for a ride last week," Lil Red voiced.

"Okay, so what happened to them. Are them niggas still alive?" I asked the silent room of females, who looked around at one other for answers.

"Now Mike, you know good damn well how them bitches operate! Hell nah, them two brothers are with their maker as we speak!" Lil Kitty blurted out as she walked into the kitchen portion of the hotel suite, smiling.

"So, how did it all go down?"
"The news people said that it was one of the most horrific crimes they had ever seen."

"Nah, Chyna!" I uttered as I stood up to look out of the window.

"Yep, it seems as though them hoes cut off them niggas dick and then placed one of them in the others mouth, while the other one got his partners dick shoved up his ass!" Chyna said as she stood there smiling.

"Damn Mike, who are these hoes?"

"Like I said before JK, I don't know."

While all that was going on, Mignon, Entyce, Nicole and your girl, Strawberry just sat there inventively listening.

"All I know is that on the way up here yesterday, Strawberry's flat ass, told Chyna that she knew how to get in touch with them hoes. The next thing we hear this morning is that them niggas were found dead off inside some hotel off of Interstate 10."

"Damn, Lil Kitty, there you go again, snitching on a bitch! Don't make me jump off in that lil thin ass of yours before tonight's Bachelor Party."

"Whatever Strawberry, girl you don't want to see Ms. Kitty."

"Y'all shut up. It won't be any of that around me. Now, was those guys inside of the club last night?"

"Yep, they were there. With the same weak ass line that they had the prior week."

"Damn!"

"What's wrong, Mike? Are you afraid that the Murder Queens are sitting in this room with us right now?"

"Nah Kizzy, I just don't want the good people of Duval County thinking that my team of ladies had anything to do with their murders. Well I guess that some of you all won't be staying here tonight. Go ahead and pack your things."

"But Mike, it's too many girls for one Bachelor Party. I thought team A was going to the Party, and Richard's team was staying here dancing at the club."

"No way am I leaving all your girls here Saneavu. I can't sit back and put you guys at risk like that. You can thank the Murder Queens for all of you going to one show. I hope there are enough guys there for you all to make enough money. Now pack your things, we're out of here in thirty minutes."

Chapter 52
Impregnated!

While they packed, I started the meeting. First thing said was, "I would like to thank you girls for sending the nice arrangement of flowers to the family."

They all stopped what they were doing and once again looked around for answers.

I was just as stunned as they were when Charlie B stood up and said. "Mike, no one from the group sent any flowers!"

"Damn, that's strange. I could've sworn that I heard that lady say from the Florida Hot Girls." I then looked over at my brother who was busy playing in Strawberry's hair.

"Firstborn, didn't you hear the lady say that those flowers were from the Florida Hot Girls?"

"Yeah, it sounded like she did," he replied as he continued playing in ole girl's hair.

I then looked out the corner of my eye and saw my conscience standing over by the window with his back turned towards me. He felt my cold evil stare in his back and then grayly turned to me and said. 'It was I who sent the lovely arrangement of flowers. They were nice, weren't they?" I stood there baffled at his emerged presence.

His face was expressionless as he said. 'That's the least I could've done, since it was I who sent her to her maker, don't you think?"

As he finished talking, I could hear the girls in the background yelling out my name.

"You cold hearted piece of shit!" I angrily replied.

"Mike, Mike!" The girls were still calling out my name.

I quickly snapped out of my funk and uttered. "Oh, I'm so sorry. I was lost there for a brief minute."

"Whatever, it looked like you were trying to talk to someone outside the window. Are you going crazy or something?

I know, you probably thought that you saw the Murder Queens coming for that ass!" Lil Red said out loud as a few of the ladies joined her in laughter.

Tameia was walking back towards me with something to drink, as I said to Lil Red and the group. "Please excuse me ladies, my mind seems to have been somewhere else."

"We can see that; it seems like you have been doing that shit a lot. Just black in and out, like your talking to someone else. But in reality your actually talking to yourself," Nicole replied with a very confused look on her face.

"I'm sorry guys, I'll do better I promise."

My conscience then walked up behind Mo Money, the new female in the group. He held a tenacious looking smile on his face as he said. "I can't wait until I get this one pregnant too."

"Nah, lil homie, I'm not getting anyone else impregnated!" I replied as he walked up beside me and whispered in my ear. 'You better think twice about that before you open your mouth. Your lil precious girl Nicole is already three weeks pregnant right fucking now!"

"What, stop lying!" I shouted.

"What? If you don't believe me, why don't you ask her for yourself, right after this silly ass meeting."

I had like fifteen girls in Jacksonville that weekend. Since they had all packed into my truck with Mignon, I placed half of them inside of the limo with Mo Money and myself. But as you guessed it, everyone wanted to ride with me.

Ten minutes later, it was decided on who would ride with who to Jasper. My main concern at the time was speaking with Nicole, but first I had to let the ladies know of the trip I had to take on Monday.

Chapter 53

World Famous Group!

It looked like most of the ladies were finished packing and waiting to take their things outside. That's when I stepped in with. "Excuse me ladies, one more thing before we close out the meeting and get on the road."

"Oh Lord, what is it now Mike?" Chyna barked as I tried to settle everyone back down.

"When we get back tomorrow, we still have Apollo South. After that, Firstborn and I will be leaving for Puerto Rico the following morning."

"For what, Mike?" Mignon asked me while looking as if I was leaving them all behind and never coming back.

"I have to attend Rhynyia's brothers funeral. I'll be down there for at least a week. In the meantime, Richard and yourself will be in charge of the crew until I return."

"Well, I guess I won't be coming to work for the next week or so," Chyna said with a lil sarcasm in her voice.

"Yep, I guess I'll be taking a short vacation as well," Charlie B said to the room of girls as they all were looking around at one another.

"C'mon guys, it's not going to be that bad, I promise."

"Whatever Mike let's just get on the road already. We'll talk about this later," Suga Bear said sounding disgusted and busted.

We checked out of the nice hotel suite around eight thirty that night headed to Jasper, Florida. Once we got onto the highway, I could sense that Nicole was highly upset with me. I had tried to ask her about being pregnant, but she brushed me off and got inside the truck with Mignon. It was fine with me that she insisted on riding with Mignon and the other girls. The only problem was the burning question inside my head. I needed answers, and I needed them immediately. I could tell that it was more to the situation, due to Mignon telling me that she had something she needed to speak to me about.

If only I would have took time out to hear what it was she had to tell me. She had briefly told me that it was something that Nicole had planned for someone dear to me. I would've done everything in my power to stop Nicole from taking another person's life, if only if I would have took the time out to hear what it was Mignon had to tell me.

We arrived in Jasper around ten thirty that night. The cars that were already lined up the spot led us to believe that it was going to be a nice turn out to the show.

All I knew was that the country ass niggas in Jasper were about to get another true taste of them bad ass females known as the world famous Florida Hot Girls. Something that they didn't experience the first time that they were there.

When we walked inside of the guy's house, it was like thirty guys already there waiting on their arrival. The first thing that this one nigga who had on some small ass glasses that were too big for his little ass face said to me was. "Hey man, where is the white girls? Did you bring any of them Snow Bunnies?" his two quite large front teeth were dangling from out of his mouth, causing him to look like the human version of Bugs Bunny.

I was trying not to laugh in the brother's face, as I replied. "I do have one nice looking Snow Bunny on the team. They had to stop for condoms. She'll be here in a few minutes along with the rest of the crew of nice tantalizing women."

He started smiling from ear to ear.

In all the years of me entertaining men and women with the Florida Hot Girls, I think he was the happiest guy that I had ever seen when I told his black ass about that Snow Bunny that was due to arrive at any minute so that she could join the world famous group.

Chapter 54
Butt Ass Naked!

Now remember how in the beginning I stated that I was real green to how things were supposed to operate while doing a Bachelor Party. Well by now I was a damn pro.

My motto was if you want to be the best at what you do, you better practice until you become perfect at it! I was about to find out just how damn good I was when we arrived at the guys house who was throwing the party.

Now the owner of the modest wood frame, three bedroom house was as country as country could be. He greeted us at the front door with some tight ass Spandex biker shorts on his tall ass. They were so damn tight that you could actually see his nuts and manhood all balled up in them as he stood in the doorway ushering the girls and I inside of his home, with the biggest country ass smile that I had ever seen. I guess the brother felt that if he showed off his merchandise inside of those tight ass shorts without being obvious about it; that it would cause the girls to desire his one on one companionship.

Wrong! Just the opposite. The girls were all laughing their ass off as they were walking in by him into his house.

Suga Bear was the first female to actually speak up when she said. "Damn homie, you might want to put all of that back in its place!"

Then it was Entyce as she barked. "Wow, well I know where all the money is at when we start dancing."

All of them had stepped inside when JK said. "Boy if you don't go put some clothes on, I'm gonna call your mamma on your lil retarded ass!"

"Girl, you know you like what you see," Peekachu said to a still shocked looking JK.

"Whatever, if he knew like I did, he would cover all those nuts up before a giant squirrel came in here and attacked his ass!" JK snapped back with.

"Alright ladies, enough of the jokes. Please get to your specific areas and dress in please. The sooner you guys dress in, the quicker I can get this damn show on the road."

"Yes boss," Nicole shouted from out of one of the rooms that she had stumbled upon.

"Whatever Nicole, just dress in," I replied to her as the host and I went to the living room area so that he could pay me what he owed.

"Hey Mike, is there anything you need me to do right now?"

"Yeah, stand by the door or in the hallway, so that none of these fellows decide that they want to see what all the ladies look like naked."

"Cool, gotcha."

"Thanks, Firstborn."

Just as soon as he had turned away, Mo Money came from around the corner and said, "Hey Mike, I really don't have anything nice to wear."

"Damn, I tell you what. Ask the one chick they call Suga Bear for something to wear. Tell her I told you to ask her."

"Thanks Mike."

"No problem." She then went to the dressing room area as I turned back towards Bubba, who really resided in Valdosta, Georgia. The place in Jasper was his second home.

"Sorry about that partner. Now let's get down to the business at hand. Were you able to get the money owed to me in ones?" He bent over and placed his hand in some type of bag and emerged with. "Yes, the balance is seven hundred dollars right?"

"Yes, my good man. So this is seven hundred in ones right?"

"Yes, just like you requested," he said to me as he smiled while handing over the large sum of money.

Not bad for a night of watching a bunch of beautiful ladies get butt ass naked.

Chapter 55
Murder Queens!

Now don't ask me why in the hell would some black woman named her damn son Bubba. He stood somewhere around six foot five and weighed a whopping three hundred and twenty-five pounds, so you could imagine how this big ass biker short wearing nigga looked to my short ass girls.

After counting up the bread, I looked to him and said, "Is everyone here that needs to be here so that we can start the show?"

He still held that ugly ass country smile on his wide greasy ass face and said, "Yep, I guess it's somewhere in the neighborhood of eighty guys here. Matter of fact, the Bachelor is over there talking with the best man."

"Cool, we'll have all the brothers take a seat and I'll get the show started."

Bubba then ran his tall, biker shorts wearing ass over to the guys standing in the corner, drinking.

I went back into the room where the girls were all getting dressed. I had just bent the corner to see Firstborn nowhere in sight. "Damn, ole hardheaded ass nigga!" I said out loud as I opened the first room door where the girls were getting dressed.

As soon as I opened the door, his ass turns around with his eyes about to pop out of his damn head.

"Yo, silly country ass nigga, I thought I asked you to stay outside and monitor the damn hallway!"

"My bad lil bro, I had to come in here and make sure my baby was doing okay."

I was so mad at the nigga when I said. "Okay James, you really trying to work your way right on out the door. Man take your watermelon shaped ass outside and watch my back!" He turned to look back in the eyes of Strawberry, who was sitting there laughing at him.

"You know what I said, after the show I'm going to punish that ass! Oh, and by the way, you better not have a dick off in your ass or pussy. Tonight, that shit belongs to me!"

"Man take your ass back outside!" I yelled as he walked by me with. "My bad lil bro, I'm right outside if you need me."

"Whatever." I closed the door and turned around to witness Mo Money standing behind the door with this lil cute outfit on. It had her lil shaved, naked vagina showing. She was looking so good that I wanted to put her lil fine ass on a biscuit and sop her up with some syrup. Chyna was standing off to the side with something on that had her pretty ass big titties showing all through her top, along with some nice ass shorts that looked like she was born in them, as tight as they were hugging her nice fine red ass.

She saw me looking over at her and winked her right eye at me.

"Don't be winking at me, bring your ass over here!"

"Excuse me ladies," she said as she walked through the crowded room of females. "Yes, Mike."

"Step outside with me."

"Oh shit, here we go again," she said as she rolled her eyes.

"Shut the door."

"Okay Mike, what is it now?"

I turned to her while still admiring how nice her titties looked.

"Mike, stop staring at them."

"Whatever, you know I can't keep my eyes off of pure beauty."

"Okay Mike, I know that you didn't bring me out here to tell me that."

"No, I didn't, Chyna. Now, why did you have to still continue to harp on that situation from last week?"

She placed her back against the wall and then said.

"Now Mike, you know if that would had happened to any of the other chicks, that you would have acted just like I did."

"Not really, Chyna. I told your ass good to get your money up front! Or at least half of it. If you would have done as I told you, none of this would be happening. Now two niggas are dead because you wanted someone to contact them damn girls called the Murder Queens!"

"Mike please, you might as well stop acting like you don't know who those bitches are! I wouldn't be surprised if those bitches aren't with us every time we leave for a show. And it wasn't me who insinuated the conversation, it was your girl Ms. Strawberry! So, if you want to be mad at someone, it's her, now can I please go back in and get dressed?"

"Yes Chyna."

She turned to walk away as I just stood there looking at how nice her ass looked.

"Everything alright, lil bro?"

I turned back towards my brother. "Nah man, with what them girls did yesterday, we might as well get ready for war. Someone is going to be coming after us and them girls known as the Murder Queens!"

Dodo!

Firstborn placed his chin in his chest and then held his head back up and said. "So, what are we going to do bro?"

"Hope and pray that it doesn't have to come to that. If it does, were just going to have to be ready. Watch the door while I check on the rest of the girls.

"Gotcha."

"Yeah, you said that the last time."

"For real lil bro, I got this. You just handle the girls."

"Cool." I walked back into the room to see Suga Bear wearing something that had all of her fat nice round ass showing out of it, as if she was inviting a brother to fuck her in the ass.

Her sidekick Peekachu had on a two dollar thong that she had picked up at Family Dollar. It was so far stuck up her lil red narrow ass that you couldn't even see the string.

Now Chief smoking head, Chazz was actually wearing a blunt as her outfit. In other words she was butt ass naked, with a blunt hanging from out of her mouth. She walked by me as if I was invisible. She didn't see me until I scared her with. "So that's what the hell you're wearing out there in front of all of them country ass niggas?"

"Yep. They'll be all right," she replied as she began to walk away from me, leaving me there waving the weed smoke out of my face.

"Okay, now when your butt naked, blunt smoking ass, don't make any money tonight, don't be mad at me. You know that you should at least cover up those fiendish looking stretch marks that are all over your stomach." her head quickly snapped around.

"Fuck that!" she said.

"Damn Chazz, you just don't get it, do you?"

She stood still while staring at me and said, "Why should I? These country ass niggas are going to be too busy sucking out of this ass and pussy to even notice my nice looking stretch marks."

I hesitated for a moment, then just walked away into the other room to check on the other ladies. I whispered to myself. "If them niggas only knew what came out of that lil nasty black ass of hers."

Now the reason I said that about ole Chazz, was due to one night, the girls and I were headed to do a show in Haines City, Florida. On the way there, ole Chazz and some of the other ladies complained about being hungry. Now one thing I always preached about was to always make sure that you ate something before traveling to a show. But this particular night, I would have to enlist a new rule whenever we did a show from that night on, because of someone always wanting something to eat, because their lil hungry ass didn't eat before leaving their home.

The nearest place for the girls to get something to eat from was Taco Bell. So I pulled up to the Taco Bell.

Before they ordered I said. "Hey, y'all really don't need to be eating no Taco Bell before the show."

"Fuck that shit Mike, I'm hungry and I want me some Taco Bell!" Chazz said to me as she started surveying the drive thru menu."

"Okay," I said as I turned back to the front. Her slim black ass proceeded and then ordered a Nacho Bell Grande. Until this very day, I don't know why in the hell her black ass ordered that damn meal.

By the time, we got to the place where the show was being held, Chazz was up in my face with.

"Hey Mike, I have to take a mean shit!"

I turned to look in her face and screamed. "Ewwwwww, what in the hell are you telling me for?" I said with a dismal expression on my face.

Little did she know at that time, but it was one of my pet peeves I had when it came to the opposite sex. I mean you couldn't fart and you damn sure couldn't have to take a shit around me, due to the instant turn off.

I have broken up with a lot of females in my lifetime, all due to pet that peeve of mine.

Many friends of mine would always say, "C'mon Mike man, a female has to pass gas and even use the bathroom at some point and time." I would always reply back with.

"Okay, she can do whatever it is that she wants to, but not around my black ass!"

While staring at Chazz with that fucked up unit on my face, she was like. "Because Mike, I don't know where the bathroom is, silly ass man!"

"First of all, I told your retarded ass not to eat that Nacho Bell Grande. But no, your lil hardheaded ass had to go ahead and do you! Now look at your silly ass, you have to doodoo!"

Chapter 56
Consumption!

She angrily looked into my eyes, with her eyes turning a dark deep brown and said. "Mike stop playing, I'm about to shit all over myself, please help me!"

"Girl you are really getting on my last nerve." I then turned to see a lil short, fat guy peeking from around the corner of the house ear hustling.

"Hey, my man, where is the restroom?"

He didn't even hesitate as he uttered. "It's over there to the right, the last room in the back." His short fat faced ass held a shitty ass grin on it, as he stood there watching Chazz sprint to the bathroom.

While she was sprinting down the hallway the lil short dude followed her into the damn bathroom and actually sat there and watched her take a dump.

"What in the hell?" I said to myself as I ventured down the hall behind the two.

I thought that maybe he was trying to pay for some sex before the show, so I wanted to make sure things were on the up and up. I was baffled as I walked to the place where he said the bathroom was. There was no door on the bathroom as Chazz was sitting there on the toilet with legs crossed. But that wasn't the odd thing, the odd thing was the damn guy was sitting next to her on the base of the bathtub.

"Hey Chazz, what in the fuck are you doing? Taking a shit or having a damn conversation!"

She looked back up at me with a sense of relief and said. "Both my nigga!"

As you guessed it, she was actually sitting there having a conversation and smoking a blunt with the guy who sat there smelling her ass because she didn't even bother to do a courtesy flush.

A few months later, that lil short guy that was sitting there that night inhaling her toxic fumes, actually got a job as the lead guy in a septic tank company. I guess you can say that he really liked smelling other people's shit.

Like I said, after that night I had to make a habit of telling the guy or woman that hired the Florida Hot Girls for a show or party, to make sure that they had food ready and available when we arrived and always during the show. We were not coming if there was no food there for our consumption.

Chapter 57
Beauty And Assets!

Lil Red's fine ass snapped me back to reality. After I had been there thinking back to that night that Chazz had the awful run in with her stomach, she was standing off to the side of the room admiring how nice she looked in her new two piece outfit that wasn't showing her stomach, nor those hideous stretch marks.

She still looked like an angel sent from heaven with what she had on, along with her cute signature smile held over her gorgeous looking face.

As I stood there gazing at her beauty, style and grace, it was somewhat bittersweet, due to her telling me earlier in the week that she would be leaving the group soon.

It seemed as though she had met some guy at the Mall in Orlando a few weeks prior to one of our shows. They had went out a few times and after a few months of dating, he realized that he couldn't live his life without her and her daughter in it.

She claimed that he played for the Cowboys and that he really loved her, and that she had actually fell in love with him. He wanted her to quit dancing so that he could take care of her and her child and that he wanted to turn her into the housewife that he had always dreamed about.

Now no one was really talking to Lil Kitty, since she was the cause of the ladies losing the Caribbean Beach Nightclub. She really didn't care, just as long as no one put their hands on her. She was fine with the silent treatment.

She just kept right on walking around the room with that cute lil smile over her face. Her outfit was a nice, lil black thong and bra set that covered up her small petite body. I really believe that she went to bed with that same look on her face nightly. She had to, because it was always the same damn smile.

Even the night that I finally got with her in the back of my truck, while sitting in her parking lot. She had that same smile on her face as I placed all of my manhood deep off inside of her small stomach.

So you see, that's why I could never fire her, she was too valuable to the team. You Beta Believe It!

Now Charlie B and her lil white waitress friend hand on the same outfit, telling the guys that they were twins.

Funny thing about that was that them country ass niggas actually believed them, especially the one guy who looked like Bugs Bunny. My Little Island Princess had to be one of the cutest females there that night, while wearing this nice one piece outfit. It was fitting her lil fine ass like a glove as she waltzed by me smelling like a bed of roses. She had stopped in front of me, while holding a genuine smile on her face and said. "You like my outfit daddy?"

"Yes, how did you know." I replied, while biting my bottom lip in approval with what she was wearing.

"Because I can see how John Boy is trying to turn into the Incredible Hulk inside of your nice ass slacks.

After the small talk with her, I looked over to see JK and her crew of females wearing all matching outfits that they had picked up from the store off of Orange Blossom Trail.

In the meantime, Mignon and Entyce both had on some Gucci type outfit that had their ass and vagina hanging out from both sides. It was mouthwatering.

Even your girl Strawberry had stepped up her wardrobe, with her red see through outfit, which displayed her natural beauty and assets.

Chapter 58
Eighth Wonder!

All of the ladies were dressed in and ready to perform, as I stood there making sure that everyone was on point and looking their best. The time had come for them to put on another one of their fabulous performances.

I stuck my head out of the door to my brother and said, "Hey, go tell the other ladies to come over here."

"Yeah, no problem Baby Boy." my brother hurriedly walked away.

Moments later, all of them were waiting on me to speak.

"Okay ladies, since you all are here and ready to make this money. I'm about give these country ass niggas the spill, so if I were you guys, I would pay closer attention to what I'm about to tell them," I uttered as all eyes and ears focused on me. Then I said, "After that, it will be your time to shine. If I were you all, I would pay close attention to what I'm about to tell these country ass brothers, so that you're sure you get your money. If any one of you ladies have a date after the show, please let me know and we'll go from there. Good luck, and have a nice night. Most of all, have fun."

As I turned to walk out of the room so that I could speak to the guys, Nicole was looking at me like if she had a knife, she would've stabbed me in the back when I waltzed past her. All the while, she was looking nice as hell with what she had adorned over her beautiful body.

My conscience, who was walking behind me whispered in my ear. "If looks could kill my brother, you would've been dead as soon as we arrived."

"Thanks, that's what your here for, to make sure that never happens. You said that you have my back, remember."

"I can only see so far into the future my good man. You have to use your six sense for the rest."

"Whatever, then what good are you here for?"

He looked at me with that evil, sinister look on his face and then said, "Be careful what you wish for, you might just see before the night is over," he replied as he placed his back up against the wall and lit his cigar.

I stood there for a minute, pondering what he meant by that comment.

I was just about to walk up and ask him, when Bubba stepped from around the corner of his small home and said, "Hey Mike, all the guys are seated and waiting for you inside of my living room."

"Thanks Bubba, I'm on my way." I gave Bubba a half ass smile and followed behind him into the living room.

The room was crowded with men sitting on top of one another, waiting for their chance to see the ladies. I was stunned at the huge number of guys as I made my way through the crowd. I had just got to the center of the room, with all eyes on me. I quickly cleared my throat and smoothly eased my balled fist away from my mouth and said. "Okay, listen up fellas, I need to have your undivided attention for a few minutes, if you all don't mind. I'm about to bring out the eighth wonder of the world. Which is, the Florida Hot Girls!"

The guy that looked like Bugs Bunny leaned over to his partner and asked him. "Hey, what is the other seven wonders of the world?"

His partner who looked as just as weird as he did, glanced back at Bugs and said. "Man, how in the hell am I supposed to know. We were both in the same special Ed class together, which means whatever you learned I learned."

Bugs just stared at his ole high school classmate and uttered. "So you're just as dumb as I am!"

"Yep!"

Chapter 59
Getting Hitched!

The small, three bedroom, wood frame house was quiet as a mouse as I stood there with all of their attention focused on what I had to say. At first, I thought that maybe it was my prestigious looking outfit, in which I had on, that caused all of their eyes to be focused on me.

I mean I was standing there dressed in a two-piece Jean outfit with a light brown FUBU shirt and light brown Timberlands to match on my feet. I was looking like a younger fresh version of Martin Lawrence.

"First, I would like to thank you all for spending your Saturday night with the Florida Hot Girls and I. You fellas could've been anywhere else in the world tonight, but you all decided on the spending the evening with the ladies and I. Before I go any further, please allow me to introduce myself. My name is Michael Vallentino and to clear one thing up real quick. I'm not a pimp to popular beliefs. I'm just the guy who brought these beautiful exotic women here for some fun and erotic entertainment.

Now there is a few things that I require you gentlemen to do tonight. The very first one and most important one is to please respect the ladies at all times. There are no bitches in here nor is there any hoes, or sluts. Just pretty ass ladies trying to get at whatever's in your pockets.

Now every female is going to come around and dance on you if that's what you require. If they are dancing on you, it's always polite to throw money their way. Not change, such as quarters or dimes and nickels. Please throw what we like to call them, green backs or better yet, big faces.

Now I have changed out a lot of you guys money so that you can have some entertainment at your beckoning call. Please don't pour any beer or alcoholic beverages inside of the females. I had a guy just a few weeks ago, pour some beer inside one of the young ladies vagina and then tried to suck it out of her. Talking about he wanted to see how pussy and beer tasted mixed up together. As if his stupid ass was trying to invent a new mixed drink or something, crazy ass nigga.

As long as you guys' respect, the ladies they will in turn respect you. Now, later on during the course of the evening, we will have our first annual Pussy eating contest. I've been told that there are some real hungry ass Eaters located back off in these parts of Florida. The winner of the contest gets to take his choice of female back home with them as the trophy."

When I said that, those country ass guys went crazy, jumping all up and down and screaming from one guy to the next. I actually heard this one brother tell his friend.

"Man, when I eat the bottom out of that one chick name Chazz, I'm taking her home to meet momma, then we getting hitched!"

Chyna was doing what she did best, being nosey. As she heard me and the guys out front yelling and laughing amongst one another, she could barely stand herself as she burst back into the room of ladies and said. "Mike is a fucking trip, he has all of them country ass dudes out there laughing their asses off. Hell I'm ready to get in them pockets!"

I have to admit, at every show I did in my fourteen year career, every one of them were always different time after time. No show was ever the same.

After all the noise and hoopla had settled down, I took control of the crowd and said. "Now without further ado, fellows please put your hands together and give it up two times for the eighth wonder of the world, the world famous, Florida Hot Girls!"

Chapter 60
Newborn Baby!

Just as I made the announcement, the ladies marched out looking like a million dollars. Lil Kitty led the way since she was the shortest female in the group. While the Island Princess, Tameia followed closely behind her. Then there was my new sex toy Ms. Mo Money, who was followed by non-other than stank booty ass Peekachu, with her red ass. The rest of the team followed behind the first line of girls, while the DJ had them all bouncing to some 2Pac. The song was Hail Mary. It brought a smile to my face to witness all of my females come out shaking their ass and making them country ass brothers beg for one of them to come dance on them.

"Man speed the damn music up!" Lil Kitty yelled to the DJ, who then threw on some Ja Rule and Ashanti, the song was Put It On Me.

The girls got so crunk off the bass line that I had to calm some of them down. That's when I happened to glance over to the right of me to see Suga Bear sitting on top of one guys face, while Peekachu had one brother taking off his clothes right along with her ass. Your girl Chazz was over in the corner of the small room with yes, for the tenth damn time, someone's blunt stuck off in her mouth.

Now my girl Mignon was dancing in the middle of the floor on the Bachelor as he made it thunderstorm on her fine ass.

Tarshay, who had now joined the group full-time, came out of the dressing room with half of her ass hanging out. I grabbed her by her the arm and said, "Damn, Tarshay, half of your ass is hanging out of your outfit!"

She looked up at me with that inviting smile of hers. "I know Mike, that's because the other half is about to be in your open mouth."

"Whatever," I replied to her as she ran to the center of the dance floor next to Mignon and started getting completely naked.

I walked away shaking my head at the sight of her, and I happened to stumble into Bubba's kitchen to see Strawberry bent over in the man's refrigerator looking for something else to eat, besides the Chicken wings and cold cut sandwiches.

The music was loud, and the guys were screaming at the top of their lungs, as I shouted. "Strawberry, what in the hell are you doing in the man's fridge. This ain't your damn house!"

She turned around looking at me as if she did live there and shouted. "Whatever Mike, them lil bitty ass wings didn't do a damn thing for my stomach!"

"Damn, so what are you going to do? Make you a full course meal?"

"No, just find something else to go with the appetizers," she replied as she bent back down, searching throughout the fridge.

"Whatever Strawberry, go ahead and do you."

"Thanks dawg," she replied as she continued to raid Bubba's fridge.

I then turned back around to catch Entyce over in the corner with one of her lovely titties stuck deep off inside some guys mouth. It actually looked as if the guy was a baby and she was breast feeding the poor guy.

Now, remember the one guy who wanted a Snow Bunny. Well his head was so far up the lil white chick's ass that it looked like she was giving birth to a newborn baby!

Chapter 61
Pencil Dick!

I just stood there laughing to myself at how those country ass brothers were reacting towards the nice array of beautiful women I had entertaining them for the night. The gorgeous, stunning looking Charlie B had three guys over in the corner, making them throw fives and tens along with a few twenties at her sexy cute ass. I had just walked up close enough for her to hear me and said.

"Damn Charlie B, you ain't playing are you?"

Her long silky hair was flying everywhere as she said. "No Michael, I'm so turned up tonight, that I feel like giving you some of this good ass pussy after the show!"

I stood there shocked as I quickly replied back with. "Damn, let's make that shit happen!"

Just as soon as I shouted that back at her, she pointed behind me.

I quickly turned to see Nicole watching me from behind the makeshift liquor bar, standing there as if she was going to pull out her four nickel and do me like she did Detective Pass.

I smiled at her and then made a B line to the patio area, where I saw Tameia dancing on top of the patio table. She had four guys standing around the table looking up at her as if she was a movie and they were paying customers all watching the same movie as she began to take off her clothing for their pleasure.

I must say, she was stunning just as much as she was beautiful. She saw me looking at her and began to take off her entire outfit. As she got butt naked for those four guys and myself, I actually think that I saw one guy trying to masturbate while standing there watching her. It wasn't until his drunk ass homie turned around to him and said, "Nigga, why do you have your short ass pencil dick out watching this female dance?"

His homie stood there with a look of guilt for a minute and then said. "Man I'm so damn drunk that my dick must have fell out of my pants!"

Tameia was on stage laughing as the comical scene unfolded and shouted. "It's so damn short that it doesn't matter if he keeps it out or not, no one is going to see it anyway!"

The rest of the small crowd started laughing as I just smiled at her and said. "Are you going to be alright out here, or do you need me to send Firstborn out here with you?"

"I'm good, bae, I'll be back in just as soon as I get the rest of my money."

"Do you, baby girl. If you need me I'm right around the corner," I replied as I walked back inside where all of the other girls were dancing.

I had just walked back inside, scanning the room looking for my favorite girl JK, who was over by the DJ standing there with her money bag entirely to full. She looked up and saw me looking at her. She then shouted over at me with. "Mike, you need to bring your lil black ass over here and change out my bag!"

"Okay, bring your fine ass back here in the dressing room," I replied.

Things were going just as planned as I walked through the crowd of guys still dancing and throwing money at all the ladies. That's when the DJ threw on some Slick Rick, the song was Children's Story the females then started dancing old school on the guys who they were dancing on. The large crowd of men went wild, right along with Firstborn, who started throwing money at the ladies as well. I was walking by him on the way to the room so that I could change JK's money bag out, when I turned to him and said, "Alright silly ass nigga, don't throw all of your damn money away trying to impress these country ass brothers up in here!"

He turned back to me and said. "Nah, this is the some of the money from them two crooked ass cops that I took for you and myself."

"Oh. You know you never told me exactly how much money you took from them two that night."

He looked back at me with that silly ass expression that he always held on his face and said. "Oh, I forgot to tell you, it was somewhere around two hundred and twenty-five thousand dollars."

My eyes enlarged at the large sum of money he said. I stared back into his eyes and uttered. "Man, you know you're a damn fool right?"

"Damn Mike, I figured that sense we're going down to Puerto Rico, we could use the money for our vacation."

"Yeah, I guess you have a point. Now let me get backso I can change out JK's ones for her. Oh before I forget, I saw your girl Strawberry over by the fridge about ten minutes ago without any money in her bag at all. You might won't to go handle that, since you're fucking her!"

Chapter 62

Hey Bubba!

His eyes, face and body began to contort as he looked back at me and said. "Man, where is she at now again. She knows how I am about that money and sweet ass pussy of hers!"

"Firstborn, please don't tell me that you have fallen in love with ole Strawberry."

"Nah, it's just that I won't to make sure that she knows who and what her purpose in the group is."

"Whatever that means homie, I'm gone man!"

As I walked back over to attend to the business at hand, Suga Bear came up to me with. "Hey Mike, I have a VIP with this guy."

"Okay Suga Bear, you didn't have to bring him to me. Whatever you decide to do is entirely up to you."

"I know, I was just letting you know in case you were looking for me."

"I understand that, but whatever you decide to do is entirely up to you. You're responsible for your own actions!"

I finally made it back to the room, where JK was already there waiting on me. I walked into the room with a smile on my face and said. "Okay JK, sorry about the wait, let me hurry up and change your ones out so I can get back to the rest of the ladies out front."

"Yeah, hurry that ass up, I was wondering what was taking your ass so damn long," she replied as she threw her bag on the bed and then began admiring herself in the full length mirror.

Moments later is when I said to her. "Here you go." I then left her in the room still admiring herself in the mirror.

I then walked back out to where the ladies were still dancing and propped myself up against the wall. I was standing there looking and desiring to be with Chyna who, was sitting over by the bar talking with Bubba and a couple of his friends. The sexy looking ass Mo Money stepped up to me and said. "Excuse me, Mike."

"Yes, beautiful one?"

She blushed and put her lil pretty head down. She then said. "Thanks for bringing me to the show."

"Don't mention it young lady. So how much money have you made so far tonight?"

"I don't know, I haven't counted it yet, but I think it's somewhere around five hundred dollars."

"Okay, well try to make another three hundred so that you can have some spending money along with some money that you can put away for a rainy day." –

"And if I make that much, how much do I owe you, Mister Mike?"

"What, I didn't tell you?"

"No," she replied as a splendid looking smile appeared across her lovely face.

"All you have to pay me is thirty dollars."

"That's it?"

"Yep, that's it, just thirty dollars."

"Now that's what I'm talking about," she replied with joy as she kissed me on my cheek and then walked away while I stood there noticing a new crowd of guys who had just walked into the party.

"What's up fellas, do you guys need some ones?" I asked them as they walked past me.

"Nah, we good playa. We're throwing nothing but big faces anyway. So, we won't need anyone's."

"Sounds good to me fellas, enjoy your night," I replied as I stood there and then shouted. "Hey Bubba, let me holla at cha for a quick second."

[]

Chapter 63
Naked As Well!

Bubba had just walked up beside me, reeking of chicken wings and someone's tart pussy that he had ate on earlier in the night. I made a point of asking him after our conversation who was the female that he dived mouth first into.

"Yeah, Mike, what's up, my man?"

"You see the guy who I just let in with three of his homies around him like their his bodyguard."

Bubba surveyed the room for a minute, after locating the young man in question, he uttered. "Oh, you talking about Rico Jones. He's cool, Mike. Ever since his parents hit the lotto, he thinks that he runs this small ass town! He's quite harmless, believe me, you have nothing to worry about."

"Cool, because I didn't won't my brother to have to pull out that chrome three eighty of his and let these.brothers see how them fools from Madville, Madison, Florida do things."

"Mike, you from Madison?" he asked with a startled look about his face.

"Yes, both me and my brother. Our family is probably the biggest family in Madison."

"Damn, you did tell me that you were from there. I have some family there also."

"Oh yeah."

"Yeah, have you ever heard of the Robinson family?" he asked as he continued to stand there smiling at the sight of all the women in attendance.

"Yeah, I have a cousin by the name of Travis "Motor" Robinson. Who knows Bubba we might be some kin and don't even know it."

A smile came as the thought resonated through his thick skull.

"Hey Bubba, one more thing before you get back over to my girl, Chyna."

"Yeah Mike, what is it?"

"I don't know how to ask you this."

"What is it Mike, go ahead bro."

"Did you eat out one of the girls earlier?"

He began to act all innocent, then it turned into laughter as he looked back at me and said. "Damn man, how did you know?"

"Damn," I mumbled to myself. "Nothing never gets by me playa. You can say that I have that intuition, when it comes to my ladies."

"Man, you're good."

"Thanks, so which one was it?"

He slowly looked around the room, when he spotted her, he leaned over and said. "Man, it was the one over there. I think she calls herself Chazz or spazz, something like that."

"Thanks, my man. Well don't let me stop you from getting back to Chyna."

"Thanks Mike, and before I forget, thanks for bringing all these females. I know that I only paid for five. I thought that you were lying when you said that you were bringing more than that."

"No problem, my man, I always aim to please. Now go ahead and enjoy yourself!"

As soon as he walked away headed back over to Chyna, I was searching the room for tart pussy smelling ass Chazz.

I was just about to walk away from the wall when the DJ threw on the song Danger by Mystikal. The girls all began to get butt naked as the song hyped them up. For a minute there, I stopped dead in my foot tracks and began to enjoy the entertainment myself, but just as soon as I hesitated to catch a glimpse at the naked beauties.

Mignon walked up behind me and whispered. "Mike, can I speak with you for a quick minute please?"

"Yeah, give me a second," I said to her as I stood there smiling at the women in front of me. I was so caught up with what my eyes were watching that Mignon just walked away and started getting naked as well.

Chapter 64
Smoked Ribs

I would later regret that I didn't find out what Mignon wanted to talk to me about that night.

Three hours later, the last guy had threw his last few dollars, so it was decided to go ahead and shut the show down. While the ladies were all inside the rooms dressing back in, Firstborn and I made the decision to drive back home. There was no need to tell the girls as one by one they all walked out to the living room area where we stood, looking like they had put in a long eight hours of work at someone's job.

After they were all dressed and assembled together, we were all walking back to the appropriate vehicle to get into with Mignon having a different demeanor covering her face.

What was it that she had to tell me? Whatever it was, I just blew it off as I climbed into the backseat of the limo, ready to get some sleep on the drive back home.

The drive home was about six hours, so we didn't stop for breakfast as I told the ladies that I would cook for them once we got back to my place. By the time that we did get back to my place, everyone was too tired to even think about breakfast, as they all searched throughout the house for somewhere to lay their sleepy head.

I was still in a good mood, since we all had such a good night, that I told the girls that I would throw a nice cookout for everyone when I woke up.

My house was packed with all seventeen girls, along with my brother and my newfound friend, Ms. Money, who of course found her lil tiny petite body in my double king sized bed, butt ass naked once again. Little did she know that when she awoke later that day, her tantalizing body would be engulfed with ten and half inches of rock-hard meat.

Now here is where things got tricky for a brother. We left Jasper, Florida around three in the morning and arrived back in Orlando around eight thirty that morning.

It was somewhere around 9:45 when I finally fell asleep. My body was so drained from being at the funeral the previous day, then traveling to Jacksonville and from there to Jasper. I hadn't had but a few hours of sleep, so my body let me sleep way too late. I finally woke up around three thirty-five that Sunday afternoon.

Everybody was still sleep as I stumbled to the kitchen and started getting things ready for my cookout. After seasoning the meat and making sure that I had everything else ready to go, I found myself outside at the grill, throwing on a few slabs of smoked ribs and some chicken. Along with some burgers and Garlic Crabs Legs.

While singing and humming to myself as I cooked on the grill, I didn't notice the elegant looking Mignon walking over to me as she finally felt as if it was the perfect time to talk to me about whatever it was she needed to speak to me about.

"Good afternoon, Mike."

She startled me as I turned to her and said, "Hey Mignon, what's on your mind, beautiful?"

Just as she fixed her mouth to say something, she looked up to see Nicole looking at the both of us from her bedroom window. I didn't see Nicole, due to my back being turned, all I saw was the expression held on the face of Mignon.

That's when I said, "Okay Mignon, go ahead, what is it?" I asked as I turned over a few slabs of the nice aroma smelling smoked ribs.

Chapter 65
Reese!

Something must have spooked her. She looked me directly in my eyes and said. "Nothing Mike, I will talk to you later."

She then quickly turned away and walked with me looking at how damn fine she was. I would often question myself as to why didn't I have her in my bed. Only time would answer that question.

Minutes later, Nicole strolled down. She placed her feet in the cool, brisk water and looked over in my direction at the grill. I looked up and caught her bitter stare, as she sat there with her head up.

After a couple of minutes of her staring at the pool, I yelled out to her. "Yo, Nicole, what are you staring at?" She looked so mad and evil.

She glanced up at me and then made a gesture with her hands, which resembled her holding her four nickel in the palms of her hands and pretended to shoot me in the chest. I fell back as if she actually shot me, when she yelled back to me.

"Think it's a game, my nigga. You have played with the wrong girl's fucking heart, Mister Michael Vallentino."

"Damn, that's how you feel?" "Mike you keep playing with all these lil female's feelings and that's what's going to happen to you!" she said to me as she got up out of the pool and walked away, swaying her thick ass hips from side to side.

As she walked away, I couldn't help but notice that she was picking up some weight in her hips. The addition looked nice on her, so I thought nothing of it as Mignon shouted out.

"Mike, that's what I've been trying to tell you."

"Tell me what Mignon?"

"Ever since you and Sharon went out to lunch the other day, she's been acting a lil strange, as if she's going through something."

"She's just tripping, she'll be alright with a lil love and tenderness," I replied while I continued cooking.

Two hours later, everyone was up and walking around the massive structure that some of the girls and I called home. Suga Bear was the first one to come up to me at the grill, sipping on her a tall glass of orange juice and gin.

"Damn dawg, so this is where the nigga that owns the world famous Florida Hot Girls, be kicking it at!"

I stood back from the grill with the tongs in my hand and said. "Yes Suga Bear, this is where that cool laid back son of bitch lives!"

"Yeah, my nigga, I see why these lil young ass broads be falling for your black ass. You all up in here living like a fucking king and shit," Peekachu said as she walked over drinking on a cold Bud Light.

"Hey, while I have you two over here together. Y'all need to check on your girl Chazz and see why her pussy is smelling a bit tart!" They both started laughing, when Suga Bear stopped she looked at me and said. "Hell, that's Reese's pussy, and I don't have a damn thing to do about that."

"Who in the hell is Reese?"

"Damn Mike, that's her name. Reese!"

"Who?"

"Chazz, silly ass nigga!" Peekachu shouted as the both of them walked away still laughing.

Chapter 66
Beep!

Two hours later, every female at my house that Sunday afternoon, were by the pool with a paper plate in one hand and a mixed drink in the other one. All while enjoying one another's company as we all feasted on some Smoked Barbecue Ribs and Chicken. Along with some nicely seasoned Garlic Crab Legs, Corn, Potatoes, Shrimp and Sausage, with some Dirty Rice, Macaroni and Cheese, Baked Beans cooked with some ground beef mixed in with it. Ah Yes, I really threw down that day for the females that the world knew as the Florida Hot Girls.

Time flew by so fast that beautiful Sunday afternoon, as the girls and I became closer than we had been before. I must admit times were good and it seemed like they were about to even get better. Only if I would've known what was about to happen to the beautiful thing that I had created called the Florida Hot Girls and I the very next day.

The ladies all danced back at Apollo South that Sunday night, even though they didn't really want to go back there on Tuesday nights, due to the crowd following them over to Hollywood Nites. I still felt like we owed Apollo South our presence since they had been so helpful to our successful start in the business.

The ladies and I had another wonderful night, in which I thought was a fitting ending to a beautiful weekend, that started with the burial of one of the group's first females. And ending with the introduction to a very beautiful newcomer who went by the name of Mo Money, who I was going to bring along just right, with my guidance and knowledge of the game in which she decided to enter.

The next day, my brother and I were at Orlando International Airport waiting for Rhynyia's father's private jet to arrive so that we could embark on a much anticipated vacation and burial of her younger brother who had been murdered a few weeks earlier, when I got the call.

"Hello."

"Is this Mike?"

"Yes, and who is this?"

"Mike, it's Karen, Sharon's mother."

"Oh hi ma'am, how are you?"

"I'm fine, is Sharon with you?"

"No ma'am, I tried to call her earlier this morning to let her know that I was leaving town for a few days, but her phone went straight to voicemail."

"Yes, I did too, Mike. I believe something very bad has happened to her!"

"Why do you say that?" I asked her as my phone began to beep.

Chapter 67
Run!

As I pulled the phone down, so I could see who was calling me, I noticed that the caller ID read private.

"Now who in the hell is this playing on my damn phone?" I mumbled to myself as I stood there with my brother.

"Hello."

"Michael Vallentino?"

"Yes, and who is this?"

"Hold on sir, let me ask the questions. You just listen."

"Man, who in the hell is this?" I asked as Firstborn turned to look at me.

"The question here sir, is do you love your beautiful looking girlfriend? And if your answer is yes, you might want to take that bass out of your voice before you have to have another one of those nice white tailored made suits did for yourself. So that you look nice for her and her daughter's funeral as well! Do I have your attention now?"

"Oh shit, please don't hurt her or her daughter!" is all I could say to the voice on the other line.

"Okay, now that I have your undivided attention, here is what we want in return for here and her lil precious daughter's life."

"Could you give me a minute while I click off of the other line with her mother?" I asked the voice on the other line.

"Sure, why not."

I immediately clicked over to my other line, sounding hysterical and in a near panic. "Ms. Karen."

"Yes Michael," she said as she seemed like she could sense the panic in my voice.

"I don't know how to tell you this."

"Go ahead, what is it, is Sharon and Breanna okay?" she asked as it seemed as if she was in a state of shock as well.

"Somewhat, Sharon and Breanna have been kidnapped."

"What, oh God no!" her mother screamed, back into the phone.

"Yes ma'am, please hold on, while I find out what their demands are." I then clicked back over to hear this badly disguised voice began to tell me what they wanted.

As they began to talk, I could hear sirens in the distance fleetly approaching the hanger where we were waiting for Rhynyia.

But just as I went to speak back into the phone, I could see five patrol cars racing towards us.

Firstborn saw the cars and acted as if he was ready to run at first sight of the patrol cars coming towards us. He then turned to me with fear and fright written all over his face and yelled. "Mike, I'm a three time felon, if I get caught with this pistol on me, I might not ever see daylight again. What are we going to do?"

I didn't know what to do, as I stood there wondering what in the hell were the patrol cars coming at us for. I just stood there stuck, with the kidnappers and Sharon's mother on the phone. I was just about to speak back into the phone when we both saw the huge twin engine private luxury jet descending from out of the big blue sky.

"Mr. Vallentino, Mr. Vallentino." I could hear the kidnappers calling my name, but all I was concerned with, was the white, red and blue colored private luxury jet plane that had just hit the runway, headed straight for me and my brother.

The jet slowly began creeping to a neutral spot away from the hangar when the doors of the private jet began to open. My conscience then stepped from around the corner of the hangar and started running towards the open door. He turned to me with his pistol already drawn and shouted. 'Run nigga, run!"

Before I knew it, Firstborn was running right behind me with our luggage in both of his hands.

Chapter 68
Their Demands!

My brother and I were running at top speed, trying to get to the entrance of the plane, when I looked up to see Rhynyia, standing at the entrance of the plane, waving her hand intensely at the both of us, all while yelling.

"Run, Michael, run. Miguel don't cut the engines off. We have to take off immediately. Maria tell Miguel to take off as soon as Michael and his partner get aboard!" I was running at full speed trying to get to that door and away from the patrol cars.

When I arrived, my brother was like five steps behind me. He was already out of breath as I reached back and pulled him onto the plane along with Rhynyia. I was laying there on the bed of the plane, huffing and puffing, so damn out of breath, when I looked up into the splendid looking face of Rhynyia.

"Thank you, baby!"

"Yes Michael, don't mention it, now what in the hell is going on now?" She closed the door of the jet, that was turning around so that we could take off.

"Let me catch my breath," I said to her as I stood to my legs and placed my right hand over one of the comfortable leather seats in her father's luxury private jet plane.

Rhynyia was standing over me, still trying to sort things out, when she looked over at my brother, and said. "So, you must be the right hand to my Michael?"

He gave her his lazy ass smile and said. "Something like that beautiful, young lady. I'm his brother. The name is James Vallentino, the third aka Firstborn."

"I'm so sorry. Michael told me about you. Please forgive me, I'm Rhynyia Santiago aka Sexy Redd."

He looked into her eyes as he took her hand.

"No problem, Sexy Redd. Baby Boy has told me all about you. It's a pleasure to finally meet you. Sorry that it's like this though."

"Not a problem, Firstborn, it is right?"

"Yes."

"I'm used to this whenever it comes to your baby brother," she said with a half-smile.

"Whatever," I said as I stood there trying to catch my breath. Looking at the both of them trying to get to one another.

While standing up, I could feel the plane ascend back into the sky, as Lt. Richards and his partner stood outside of their police issued black sedan screaming for us not to take-off.

Now, while during the course of running towards the plane, the kidnappers must've hung up the phone, because I could still hear Sharon's mother in the background of my phone.

"Ms. Karen, let me call you back when I find out their demands."

"Michael, get my daughter. I've already lost one daughter, and I don't won't to lose another one!"

"Yes ma'am, as soon as I find out what's going on, I will call you back with the information." Just as soon as I hung the phone up with Karen, my phone rang. "Hello."

"If you want to see Sharon and her child ever again, alive and breathing. You will do as I say Mister Vallentino."

I fell into the plush leather couch that was inside the jet plane, with my head down, as Rhynyia sat beside me rubbing my throbbing head.

"Was this what Mignon was trying to tell me all weekend? Why didn't I take the time out to find out what it was that she wanted?" I asked myself as I sat there ready to hear their demands.

All I knew if it was, it didn't matter now. Sharon and Breanna were gone and I was the only one who could bring them back.

At least that's what the kidnappers thought. But little did they know, I had one card left in my hand and that one card was those bad ass females who called themselves, the Murder Queens.

Lock Down Publications and Ca$h Presents
Assisted Publishing Packages

BASIC PACKAGE $499 Editing Cover Design Formatting	UPGRADED PACKAGE $800 Typing Editing Cover Design Formatting
ADVANCE PACKAGE $1,200 Typing Editing Cover Design Formatting Copyright registration Proofreading Upload book to Amazon	LDP SUPREME PACKAGE $1,500 Typing Editing Cover Design Formatting Copyright registration Proofreading Set up Amazon account Upload book to Amazon Advertise on LDP, Amazon and Facebook Page

***Other services available upon request.
Additional charges may apply

Lock Down Publications
P.O. Box 944
Stockbridge, GA 30281-9998
Phone: 470 303-9761

Submission Guideline

Submit the first three chapters of your completed manuscript to ldpsubmissions@gmail.com, subject line: Your book's title. The manuscript must be in a .doc file and sent as an attachment. Document should be in Times New Roman, double spaced and in size 12 font. Also, provide your synopsis and full contact information. If sending multiple submissions, they must each be in a separate email.

Have a story but no way to send it electronically? You can still submit to LDP/Ca$h Presents. Send in the first three chapters, written or typed, of your completed manuscript to:

LDP: Submissions Dept
Po Box 944
Stockbridge, Ga 30281

DO NOT send original manuscript. Must be a duplicate.

Provide your synopsis and a cover letter containing your full contact information.

Thanks for considering LDP and Ca$h Presents.

NEW RELEASES

SOSA GANG 2 by ROMELL TUKES
KINGZ OF THE GAME 7 by PLAYA RAY
SKI MASK MONEY 2 by RENTA
BORN IN THE GRAVE 3 by SELF MADE TAY
LOYALTY IS EVERYTHING 3 by MOLOTTI

Coming Soon from Lock Down Publications/Ca$h Presents

BLOOD OF A BOSS **VI**
SHADOWS OF THE GAME II
TRAP BASTARD II
By Askari
LOYAL TO THE GAME **IV**
By T.J. & Jelissa
TRUE SAVAGE **VIII**
MIDNIGHT CARTEL IV
DOPE BOY MAGIC IV
CITY OF KINGZ III
NIGHTMARE ON SILENT AVE II
THE PLUG OF LIL MEXICO II
CLASSIC CITY II
By Chris Green
BLAST FOR ME **III**
A SAVAGE DOPEBOY III
CUTTHROAT MAFIA III
DUFFLE BAG CARTEL VII
HEARTLESS GOON VI
By Ghost
A HUSTLER'S DECEIT III
KILL ZONE II
BAE BELONGS TO ME III
TIL DEATH II
By Aryanna
KING OF THE TRAP III
By T.J. Edwards
GORILLAZ IN THE BAY V
3X KRAZY III
STRAIGHT BEAST MODE III
De'Kari

KINGPIN KILLAZ IV
STREET KINGS III
PAID IN BLOOD III
CARTEL KILLAZ IV
DOPE GODS III
Hood Rich
SINS OF A HUSTLA II
ASAD
YAYO V
Bred In The Game 2
S. Allen
THE STREETS WILL TALK II
By Yolanda Moore
SON OF A DOPE FIEND III
HEAVEN GOT A GHETTO III
SKI MASK MONEY III
By Renta
LOYALTY AIN'T PROMISED III
By Keith Williams
I'M NOTHING WITHOUT HIS LOVE II
SINS OF A THUG II
TO THE THUG I LOVED BEFORE II
IN A HUSTLER I TRUST II
By Monet Dragun
QUIET MONEY IV
EXTENDED CLIP III
THUG LIFE IV
By Trai'Quan
THE STREETS MADE ME IV
By Larry D. Wright
IF YOU CROSS ME ONCE III
ANGEL V
By Anthony Fields
THE STREETS WILL NEVER CLOSE IV
By K'ajji
HARD AND RUTHLESS III

KILLA KOUNTY IV
By Khufu
MONEY GAME III
By Smoove Dolla
JACK BOYS VS DOPE BOYS IV
A GANGSTA'S QUR'AN V
COKE GIRLZ II
COKE BOYS II
LIFE OF A SAVAGE V
CHI'RAQ GANGSTAS V
SOSA GANG III
BRONX SAVAGES II
BODYMORE KINGPINS II
By Romell Tukes
MURDA WAS THE CASE III
Elijah R. Freeman
AN UNFORESEEN LOVE IV
BABY, I'M WINTERTIME COLD III
By Meesha

QUEEN OF THE ZOO III
By Black Migo
CONFESSIONS OF A JACKBOY III
By Nicholas Lock
KING KILLA II
By Vincent "Vitto" Holloway
BETRAYAL OF A THUG III
By Fre$h
THE MURDER QUEENS III
By Michael Gallon
THE BIRTH OF A GANGSTER III
By Delmont Player
TREAL LOVE II
By Le'Monica Jackson
FOR THE LOVE OF BLOOD III

By Jamel Mitchell
RAN OFF ON DA PLUG II
By Paper Boi Rari
HOOD CONSIGLIERE III
By Keese
PRETTY GIRLS DO NASTY THINGS II
By Nicole Goosby
PROTÉGÉ OF A LEGEND III
LOVE IN THE TRENCHES II
By Corey Robinson
IT'S JUST ME AND YOU II
By Ah'Million
FOREVER GANGSTA III
By Adrian Dulan
GORILLAZ IN THE TRENCHES II
By SayNoMore
THE COCAINE PRINCESS VIII
By King Rio
CRIME BOSS II
Playa Ray
LOYALTY IS EVERYTHING III
Molotti
HERE TODAY GONE TOMORROW II
By Fly Rock
REAL G'S MOVE IN SILENCE II
By Von Diesel
GRIMEY WAYS IV
By Ray Vinci

Michael Gallon

Available Now

RESTRAINING ORDER **I & II**
By CA$H & Coffee
LOVE KNOWS NO BOUNDARIES **I II & III**
By Coffee
RAISED AS A GOON I, II, III & IV
BRED BY THE SLUMS I, II, III
BLAST FOR ME I & II
ROTTEN TO THE CORE I II III
A BRONX TALE I, II, III
DUFFLE BAG CARTEL I II III IV V VI
HEARTLESS GOON I II III IV V
A SAVAGE DOPEBOY I II
DRUG LORDS I II III
CUTTHROAT MAFIA I II
KING OF THE TRENCHES
By Ghost
LAY IT DOWN **I & II**
LAST OF A DYING BREED I II
BLOOD STAINS OF A SHOTTA I & II III
By Jamaica
LOYAL TO THE GAME I II III
LIFE OF SIN I, II III
By TJ & Jelissa
BLOODY COMMAS I & II
SKI MASK CARTEL I II & III
KING OF NEW YORK I II,III IV V
RISE TO POWER I II III
COKE KINGS I II III IV V
BORN HEARTLESS I II III IV
KING OF THE TRAP I II
By T.J. Edwards
IF LOVING HIM IS WRONG…I & II
LOVE ME EVEN WHEN IT HURTS I II III

By Jelissa
WHEN THE STREETS CLAP BACK I & II III
THE HEART OF A SAVAGE I II III IV
MONEY MAFIA I II
LOYAL TO THE SOIL I II III
By Jibril Williams
A DISTINGUISHED THUG STOLE MY HEART I II
& III
LOVE SHOULDN'T HURT I II III IV
RENEGADE BOYS I II III IV
PAID IN KARMA I II III
SAVAGE STORMS I II III
AN UNFORESEEN LOVE I II III
BABY, I'M WINTERTIME COLD I II
By Meesha
A GANGSTER'S CODE I &, II III
A GANGSTER'S SYN I II III
THE SAVAGE LIFE I II III
CHAINED TO THE STREETS I II III
BLOOD ON THE MONEY I II III
A GANGSTA'S PAIN I II III
By J-Blunt
PUSH IT TO THE LIMIT
By Bre' Hayes
BLOOD OF A BOSS I, II, III, IV, V
SHADOWS OF THE GAME
TRAP BASTARD
By Askari
THE STREETS BLEED MURDER **I, II & III**
THE HEART OF A GANGSTA I II& III
By Jerry Jackson
CUM FOR ME I II III IV V VI VII VIII
An LDP Erotica Collaboration
BRIDE OF A HUSTLA **I II & II**
THE FETTI GIRLS **I, II& III**
CORRUPTED BY A GANGSTA I, II III, IV

BLINDED BY HIS LOVE
THE PRICE YOU PAY FOR LOVE I, II ,III
DOPE GIRL MAGIC I II III
By Destiny Skai
WHEN A GOOD GIRL GOES BAD
By Adrienne
THE COST OF LOYALTY I II III
By Kweli
A GANGSTER'S REVENGE **I II III & IV**
THE BOSS MAN'S DAUGHTERS I II III IV V
A SAVAGE LOVE **I & II**
BAE BELONGS TO ME I II
A HUSTLER'S DECEIT I, II, III
WHAT BAD BITCHES DO I, II, III
SOUL OF A MONSTER I II III
KILL ZONE
A DOPE BOY'S QUEEN I II III
TIL DEATH
By Aryanna
A KINGPIN'S AMBITON
A KINGPIN'S AMBITION **II**
I MURDER FOR THE DOUGH
By Ambitious
TRUE SAVAGE I II III IV V VI VII
DOPE BOY MAGIC I, II, III
MIDNIGHT CARTEL I II III
CITY OF KINGZ I II
NIGHTMARE ON SILENT AVE
THE PLUG OF LIL MEXICO II
CLASSIC CITY
By Chris Green
A DOPEBOY'S PRAYER
By Eddie "Wolf" Lee
THE KING CARTEL **I, II & III**
By Frank Gresham

THESE NIGGAS AIN'T LOYAL **I, II & III**
By Nikki Tee
GANGSTA SHYT **I II &III**
By CATO
THE ULTIMATE BETRAYAL
By Phoenix
Boss'n Up i , ii & IIi
By Royal Nicole
I LOVE YOU TO DEATH
By Destiny J
I RIDE FOR MY HITTA
I STILL RIDE FOR MY HITTA
By Misty Holt
LOVE & CHASIN' PAPER
By Qay Crockett
TO DIE IN VAIN
SINS OF A HUSTLA
By ASAD
BROOKLYN HUSTLAZ
By Boogsy Morina
BROOKLYN ON LOCK I & II
By Sonovia
GANGSTA CITY
By Teddy Duke
A DRUG KING AND HIS DIAMOND I & II III
A DOPEMAN'S RICHES
HER MAN, MINE'S TOO I, II
CASH MONEY HO'S
THE WIFEY I USED TO BE I II
PRETTY GIRLS DO NASTY THINGS
By Nicole Goosby
TRAPHOUSE KING **I II & III**
KINGPIN KILLAZ I II III
STREET KINGS I II
PAID IN BLOOD **I II**
CARTEL KILLAZ I II III

DOPE GODS I II
By Hood Rich
LIPSTICK KILLAH **I, II, III**
CRIME OF PASSION I II & III
FRIEND OR FOE I II III
By Mimi
STEADY MOBBN' **I, II, III**
THE STREETS STAINED MY SOUL I II III
By Marcellus Allen
WHO SHOT YA **I, II, III**
SON OF A DOPE FIEND I II
HEAVEN GOT A GHETTO I II
SKI MASK MONEY I II
Renta
GORILLAZ IN THE BAY **I II III IV**
TEARS OF A GANGSTA I II
3X KRAZY I II
STRAIGHT BEAST MODE I II
DE'KARI
TRIGGADALE I II III
MURDAROBER WAS THE CASE I II
Elijah R. Freeman
GOD BLESS THE TRAPPERS I, II, III
THESE SCANDALOUS STREETS I, II, III
FEAR MY GANGSTA I, II, III IV, V
THESE STREETS DON'T LOVE NOBODY I, II
BURY ME A G I, II, III, IV, V
A GANGSTA'S EMPIRE I, II, III, IV
THE DOPEMAN'S BODYGAURD I II
THE REALEST KILLAZ I II III
THE LAST OF THE OGS I II III
Tranay Adams
THE STREETS ARE CALLING
Duquie Wilson
MARRIED TO A BOSS I II III

The Murder Queens 4

By Destiny Skai & Chris Green
KINGZ OF THE GAME I II III IV V VI VII
CRIME BOSS
Playa Ray
SLAUGHTER GANG I II III
RUTHLESS HEART I II III
By Willie Slaughter
FUK SHYT
By Blakk Diamond
DON'T F#CK WITH MY HEART I II
By Linnea
ADDICTED TO THE DRAMA I II III
IN THE ARM OF HIS BOSS II
By Jamila
YAYO I II III IV
A SHOOTER'S AMBITION I II
BRED IN THE GAME
By S. Allen
TRAP GOD I II III
RICH $AVAGE I II III
MONEY IN THE GRAVE I II III
By Martell Troublesome Bolden
FOREVER GANGSTA I II
GLOCKS ON SATIN SHEETS I II
By Adrian Dulan
TOE TAGZ I II III IV
LEVELS TO THIS SHYT I II
IT'S JUST ME AND YOU
By Ah'Million
KINGPIN DREAMS I II III
RAN OFF ON DA PLUG
By Paper Boi Rari
CONFESSIONS OF A GANGSTA I II III IV
CONFESSIONS OF A JACKBOY I II
By Nicholas Lock
I'M NOTHING WITHOUT HIS LOVE

SINS OF A THUG
TO THE THUG I LOVED BEFORE
A GANGSTA SAVED XMAS
IN A HUSTLER I TRUST
By Monet Dragun
CAUGHT UP IN THE LIFE I II III
THE STREETS NEVER LET GO I II III
By Robert Baptiste
NEW TO THE GAME I II III
MONEY, MURDER & MEMORIES I II III
By Malik D. Rice
LIFE OF A SAVAGE I II III IV
A GANGSTA'S QUR'AN I II III IV
MURDA SEASON I II III
GANGLAND CARTEL I II III
CHI'RAQ GANGSTAS I II III IV
KILLERS ON ELM STREET I II III
JACK BOYZ N DA BRONX I II III
A DOPEBOY'S DREAM I II III
JACK BOYS VS DOPE BOYS I II III
COKE GIRLZ
COKE BOYS
SOSA GANG I II
BRONX SAVAGES
BODYMORE KINGPINS
By Romell Tukes
LOYALTY AIN'T PROMISED I II
By Keith Williams
QUIET MONEY I II III
THUG LIFE I II III
EXTENDED CLIP I II
A GANGSTA'S PARADISE
By Trai'Quan
THE STREETS MADE ME I II III
By Larry D. Wright

THE ULTIMATE SACRIFICE I, II, III, IV, V, VI
KHADIFI
IF YOU CROSS ME ONCE I II
ANGEL I II III IV
IN THE BLINK OF AN EYE
By Anthony Fields
THE LIFE OF A HOOD STAR
By Ca$h & Rashia Wilson
THE STREETS WILL NEVER CLOSE I II III
By K'ajji
CREAM I II III
THE STREETS WILL TALK
By Yolanda Moore
NIGHTMARES OF A HUSTLA I II III
By King Dream
CONCRETE KILLA I II III
VICIOUS LOYALTY I II III
By Kingpen
HARD AND RUTHLESS I II
MOB TOWN 251
THE BILLIONAIRE BENTLEYS I II III
REAL G'S MOVE IN SILENCE
By Von Diesel
GHOST MOB
Stilloan Robinson
MOB TIES I II III IV V VI
SOUL OF A HUSTLER, HEART OF A KILLER I II
GORILLAZ IN THE TRENCHES
By SayNoMore
BODYMORE MURDERLAND I II III
THE BIRTH OF A GANGSTER I II
By Delmont Player
FOR THE LOVE OF A BOSS
By C. D. Blue
MOBBED UP I II III IV
THE BRICK MAN I II III IV V

Michael Gallon

THE COCAINE PRINCESS I II III IV V VI VII
By King Rio
KILLA KOUNTY I II III IV
By Khufu
MONEY GAME I II
By Smoove Dolla
A GANGSTA'S KARMA I II III
By FLAME
KING OF THE TRENCHES I II III
 by GHOST & TRANAY ADAMS
QUEEN OF THE ZOO I II
By Black Migo
GRIMEY WAYS I II III
By Ray Vinci
XMAS WITH AN ATL SHOOTER
By Ca$h & Destiny Skai
KING KILLA
By Vincent "Vitto" Holloway
BETRAYAL OF A THUG I II
By Fre$h
THE MURDER QUEENS I II
By Michael Gallon
TREAL LOVE
By Le'Monica Jackson
FOR THE LOVE OF BLOOD I II
By Jamel Mitchell
HOOD CONSIGLIERE I II
By Keese
PROTÉGÉ OF A LEGEND I II
LOVE IN THE TRENCHES
By Corey Robinson
BORN IN THE GRAVE I II III
By Self Made Tay
MOAN IN MY MOUTH
By XTASY

The Murder Queens 4

TORN BETWEEN A GANGSTER AND A GEN-
TLEMAN
By J-BLUNT & Miss Kim
LOYALTY IS EVERYTHING I II
Molotti
HERE TODAY GONE TOMORROW
By Fly Rock
PILLOW PRINCESS
By S. Hawkins

Michael Gallon
BOOKS BY LDP'S CEO, CA$H

TRUST IN NO MAN
TRUST IN NO MAN 2
TRUST IN NO MAN 3
BONDED BY BLOOD
SHORTY GOT A THUG
THUGS CRY
THUGS CRY 2
THUGS CRY 3
TRUST NO BITCH
TRUST NO BITCH 2
TRUST NO BITCH 3
TIL MY CASKET DROPS
RESTRAINING ORDER
RESTRAINING ORDER 2
IN LOVE WITH A CONVICT
LIFE OF A HOOD STAR
XMAS WITH AN ATL SHOOTER